CRYPTIC

BY DA CHANEY

Cryptic
©2011 May December Publications LLC

Second Edition
The split-tree logo is a registered trademark of May December Publications LLC

Printed in the U.S.A.

ISBN - 978-1-936730-12-4

ACKNOWLEDGMENTS

I have a lot of people to thank. I tried to keep it short, but the names just kept coming and in the end I probably missed some important people that I'll kick myself over forgetting later. For this list I was selective, but it still ended up being a long list. No one truly writes in a bubble. These people have given me so much encouragement and enthusiasm that it has stood out for me through the years. So, it's my turn to THANK YOU for you... for everything.

Theresa Marzullo, Kristopher Torres, Jonathan Carroll, Tony Schaab, Robin Coleman, Julie Velez, Alina Pasca Decker, Darren Bracey, Marlene Ullman, Renee DeSantis, Josie Toner, Christopher Wooliver, Andrew Brown, Amanda Watson, Shauna McAllister, Joan Devoe-Moors, Denise and Todd Brown, Matthew and Kristina Williamson, Sean and Becca Anderson, Patricia and Doyle Watts, and Alexis and David Keeler.

Of course, I wouldn't be who I am today without my strong family: Sandie, Ryan, James, Scott, Jeanne, Trisha, Alisha, Jaryd, Alex, Marissa, the Hassan's, and the Massaro's.

DEDICATION

This is for me.

I showed myself that I can do this. You all helped me do this, but I had to write it. It took more time than I'd intended and hopefully I can improve on that next time but I've done something that I've always wanted to do. And I ask you: How *awesome* is that? There's no magic. Just work. And a lot of editing.

I hope that you enjoy my blood, sweat, and tears.

-DAC 2011

PROLOGUE

Outskirts of the Somerset estate, English countryside, 1612

Marcus was kneeling in his own blood.

It wasn't unlike him to travel at night, but a part of him probably should have known something like this might happen one day, and maybe a part of him deep down inside, did. If he was being honest with himself, perhaps this was the thing that he had been waiting for all along. It was difficult not to think about all those empty nights of searching, when in the end it might have been for an event so simple.

There was something in the way the air smelled; crisp, cold, and unquestionably honest. Then there was the anonymity of the night shadows' ability to wrap around him like a lover and allow him to disappear entirely, that drew him out like a suicidal moth to an open flame. A kind of calling; darkly uninhibited—primal, even. When the moon shone so bright through the windows, it had an effect that beckoned to him like a seductress to a man too weak to negotiate terms. No willpower to speak of. Just a man filled with an insatiable wanting.

The completion of a brand new crypt built for his deceased relatives on the far end of his estate left him wholly on edge; like the feeling of fire ants walking across his naked shoulders, no matter what he wore and no matter how many times he scrubbed at his skin to erase the feeling. He was familiar with the sensation of uneasiness, but he had expected the feeling to actually lessen. The structure was done. He could finally take a rest now, right? Finally put quality time into the training and upbringing of his children, right? To shake the weight he'd lived with for so long?

Well, that had been the idea five years ago when he'd commissioned it to be built, anyway; that his family honor could then finally be appeased. Also, when the last stone was placed and his family was laid to rest, he could finally forgive himself. He could stop letting how he felt about his father dying because of him, rule his every action...right?

He was clearly asking the wrong man, because he didn't certainly feel the slightest *bit* appeased. The remaining invisible ants were a testament to that. Marcus had truly thought that by completing this project that his guilt would evaporate. It had felt like the clearest move that he could make. So why hadn't it?

It'd been his own fears as an eight-year-old boy that had lead his father out onto their estate grounds the night that he'd been killed. His father had been mauled to death by a wild animal and subsequently bled out alone during the night, found by staff in the early hours of morning. That very day, a hunting party tracked, killed, and brought back the beasts hideous head, but nothing had been the same ever since. It was something Marcus would never let himself truly forget, even if he wanted to feel absolved over it. His profound and lasting grief had been the shattering of his innocence. It was replaced with a choking cloud of guilt and the haunting need for atonement.

Marcus knew as a rational man that a young boy, like he had been, could not be held responsible. His perspective had changed from boy to man, as well it should have. He knew his guilt was irrational. If he had to give up his own life to defend the life of his five-year-old son, Tobias, it would be done in a heartbeat—without a second thought.

It didn't escape his attention that even though he knew this to be true, he still was unable to forgive himself for the death of his own father. In fact, it could be said that he punished himself because he knew there was no way to take it back. If he had just stayed in his bed that night and not reported the shadows he'd seen from his window, his Father might still be alive today. It was his own fear and quick move to *demand* action that had caused his father's death. Why had he been so unyielding? He still did not accept that his age had been a factor.

That night, standing there staring at the moon, the pressure in his chest was too much to bear and he wondered what *else* he would have to do to feel the weight lifted. What else could he do to make up for a bad decision that ultimately destroyed him? The grief was killing him and ruining his relationship with his wife and children. So, he left the warmth of his bed, saddled his stallion, War, and rode out into the night alone. Sleep had been impossible.

Marcus was traveling at a leisurely pace along the James Bradford road when the trouble that would change his family's life forever happened. Something had run out from a thicket of shaded trees and broadsided his horse with a brute force that was jarring to both mount and rider. Marcus caught a quick flash of the two-legged figure right itself and then bound away. It wasn't enough to truly see the man in the bad lighting, but it was enough to make out that he was running on two legs and not four. His mind quickly identified the movement as human and not animal in nature.

Startled, fingers tightening on the reins, Marcus heard War issue a startled high-pitched squeal at the same time, and with the motion of the collision carrying momentum, War managed to buck Marcus from his back. Marcus tried to grab for the reins but managed to miss them as they danced away from his fingertips. He fell backwards, landing hard on the well traveled dirt road watching stars spin above him for a moment as War bolted away like the Devil was chasing him. Marcus sat in a daze as he listened to War's retreating noise. The whole interaction was an uncharacteristic thing for the stallion to do.

In fact, it was the complete opposite of what War had been taught to do. Marcus ought to know since he'd trained side by side for hours with the foal taking his lumps each time War threw him. It hadn't been an easy lesson for either of them to learn. He wondered what in blazes had scared War so badly that he'd not only buck him but also ride off without him. He couldn't help feel anger at his trusted stead's abandonment in the middle of the night like that. It didn't seem possible that War would disobey the training, but there Marcus was, sitting on his backside watching it happen.

Cheeks burning, he shook his head and went about trying to pick himself up from the ground. It'd be a long walk home. Marcus dusted off the seat of his trousers before coming full height, when someone darted out from the darkness, running low, slashed at him, and ran away giggling. At first he hadn't known what had happened. An icy thread of cold seared a twin path along his stomach and chest for a moment before the realization set in and agonizing pain lanced through his mid-section. He shouted out, grasping his middle and prodded to see how deep the wound was. The slimy slick feeling of his guts was nothing compared to the feeling of finding that his fingers had found the deep and penetrable vertical line to start with.

Shocked, Marcus dropped to his knees heavily as he felt his warm blood gush and sluice down and over the fabric of his trousers. The smell wafted up his nose as he grunted and groaned trying to hold himself together. Sheer force of will made him stay kneeling instead of falling over, as he wondered if he'd been sliced open with a scythe. The wound across his chest felt shallow but stung against the cool night air as it also bled openly. His eyes grew hazy as he pressed one hand against his middle and retrieved a short flintlock from his side. Determined to make a stand, he shakily held the weapon out in front of him in hopes to catch sight of the man who had signed his death warrant. He pushed thoughts of Tobias and his daughters out of his mind, adamant on not losing focus. There was nothing he could do for his children now.

He couldn't help the shaking, try as he might. It wasn't that he was scared to die. He'd grown up under the ideal that a Lord would always die young one way or another and it was unlikely that he would grow a single grey hair before he met his end. No, it was the blood loss that had started a chain reaction in his body and he was losing the strength to hold the weapon up high. He locked his arm into his shoulder, pushing his elbow into the muscle of his chest and waited.

The thought had crossed his mind to press the flintlock against his temple and end it all before his attacker appeared. The idea had so much merit that he could almost feel the barrel against his skin already. Marcus forced himself to focus his attention to his wound as his blood continued to flow between his fingers. He pressed his lids closed momentarily to think.

He thought they might stay closed forever, because the sensation to lay down was so strong. He knew that the maneuver would effectively steal any further pleasure from his attacker away, but he couldn't quit yet. There was still some time before he bled out or took pity on himself and pulled the trigger to see who was behind it. Family or stranger? He had to know before he met his death.

It did not take long to wait for the culprit to emerge, and if Marcus had been smart he would have shot immediately, but something was wrong with the man and it was confused him. Seemingly not caring that Marcus held a gun, he wore no clothes and where his body wasn't cast in shadows, he was stark white. He was a man...but wasn't a man. It didn't seem possible.

The face of the figure was malformed; one side larger than the other and angled at an odd way but Marcus couldn't see the features. There was no mistaking that he was male either, as oversized glands bounced easily against his thighs. The rib cage was highly pronounced, sticking out under the light of the moon. The top half of his legs were skinny, from thigh to knee cap, but became muscular along its calves.

Trying to aim well with his one loaded shot, Marcus fired. The resounding force made him falter as he jerked the weapon awkwardly and almost fell over. Struggling to right himself, Marcus saw that the shot missed and startled the badly formed man. Enraged, the figure leapt at Marcus driving him down forcefully, sinking teeth into his shoulder as sharp fingernails dug into his forearms as they landed in a heap upon the dirt. Up close the smell of the man-like thing was horrendous. Smelling half rotten like old broccoli mixed with a decade of body odor, the stench was sickly strong and putrid and made Marcus' eyes sting.

Gagging, Marcus raised the metal reinforced butt of the thick flintlock and repeatedly struck the back of his attacker's head, but the figure only tightened his painful grip. Marcus' strength was fading fast the creature lifted its head from the bite wound and began to beat his head violently against the ground. As if trying to crack open a tough nut. The figure's heels dug into Marcus' hip bones but Marcus only half felt it. He was aware of the motion but blissfully the pain had been replaced with a sense of dulled awareness. His tongue lolled in his mouth slapping against his teeth as his head continued to be pounded into the ground. The shocking wounds of the night were taking their toll and he felt himself accept his death. He wasn't fully aware when he heard the sound of wagon wheels coming down the road toward them but he was too far gone to do much about it.

Marcus fell limp, head crooked above his neck, as the figure let him go with a vicious shove. His body jerked as the figure kicked him but he still felt no physical pain. He heard the attacker move around him towards his feet. Marcus stared up at the stars as he felt himself being jerkily dragged from the road. *Drag, stop, drag, stop.* His head thumped against dips and rocks in the ground as he was pulled along. As the sounds began to fade from his ears, he finally realized what he had to do to escape the burden of guilt. Die.

PART 1

1

Bordering the Lockland Estate, English countryside, 1716

Lost in troubled thoughts, Guliana stared vacantly from the carriage window at the foliage just beyond reach. Glistening droplets stuck to the lush cluster of leaves and colorful berries like liquid diamonds dispensed from Heaven itself. Her gaze rested on them as they flickered in fleeting rays of sunlight that poked through the overcast clouds above. Stifling a sigh, she admired the beauty in the presentation, but was aware that the drops clung quivering to the edges like frightfully desperate things. As if they feared the long fall to the ground.

Guliana knew that raindrops did not actually 'feel' anything and that her thoughts were just a mental projection of her own childish imagination brought on by her fears. Though none of it stopped her mind from playing out those imagined events as she watched a drop fall and splatter against the green blades below. She was acutely aware that there was a heavy feeling inside herself that desired to grab hold of the familiarity of her past before she plummeted headlong into the unknown of her future.

There was no denying that the silent, nagging question begged to be answered. Am I ready to be married? Little else caused her emotions to be so muddied within herself. Was she ready? The simple truth of the matter was…she couldn't be sure. How could she know if she were ready if she hadn't tried it yet? But to try it, meant to do it. And to do it meant there was no going back once she did it. It was a plaguing line of thinking that often kept her awake through the night. The finality of it all scared her to bits. What if she was stuck with someone she didn't fancy over the years? People didn't talk about it but there was little denying some marriage matches were not well aligned. She'd seen it often growing up because she made it a habit to study the people around her; the people who were to be her examples to live by. The emotions left unsaid that spoke all too well on Father's face.

There was no one she could talk to about any of this without betraying her feelings. She was expected to be married, the sooner the better. No questions asked. In fact, Mother had all but pushed her into a carriage with this man, adding her chaperone only as a fleeting afterthought. Traveling without one was simply unheard of but it nearly didn't stop Mother from arranging it.

Mother was big on risky actions that tended to bear the fruit of success birthed from her focused ambitions. She was single-handedly lucky that way. When she was a young girl, she had married off all of her single sisters after Grandmother passed away. She told the story with pride. Mother was known in small circles for catching her sisters in publicly questionable circumstances to get the couple to marry.

Her skill in getting what she wanted met with stubborn resistance in Guliana. Though even a fool could tell Mother's already limited patience was threadbare. Mother was determined and becoming more insistent. It wouldn't be long before Guliana could expect to find herself married to an aged bald man with chronic halitosis if she didn't get with the agenda soon. That all encompassing female agenda. To grow up, find a man, be married, and have children. To her irritation, sly remarks about her age made Guliana suspect that Mother couldn't wait any longer to see her belly thick with a grandchild or five to lavish affection on.

Shoulders sagging, she breathed in deep. Truly, there was little help for her raging indecisive emotions. It was her duty...her lot in life. Who was she to go against the grain of society? She'd always done what she was told to do and now would be no different. At least he was handsome enough and had money. Things could be worse.

Cryptic

Maybe it was for the best that someone else was pushing her into the decision so that she didn't have to blame herself if something went wrong. She'd blame Mother.

2

He watched Ms. Guliana Robbinbury closely, inspecting the expression on her face with calm speculation. She was distracted. Edgy, even. It was something in the way her lips turned down slightly at the corners, the hard curve of her chin, and the way her eyelids fluttered as she stared out and decidedly away from the carriage. He took it all in as his gaze swept over her body, angled as it was away from him, and he couldn't help the niggling feeling that she was displeased with him in some way.

Conor couldn't fathom what he might have done to make her withdraw the way she had, and his mind struggled to find some obvious point that he'd missed. He backtracked in his mind trying to remember something that he might have said wrong. That he didn't know much about women other than to charm them from their clothes was often a popular topic amongst his brothers. Once clothes were shed there was no real need to talk of anything, which suited him all the more. It took extra effort on his part to actually get to know a woman who preferred, for all appearances, to want to keep her clothes on. She hadn't even let him kiss her, which puzzled him, because most girls—even the chaste ones—let him tease kisses from their lips in secret. This new one preferred conversation, and so he tried to indulge her, deep in foreign territory.

It wouldn't be a cliché to say that Conor was happiest chasing single women around looking for a good time, because that's exactly what he liked. His more physically attractive brothers had less romantic trouble with the ladies than Conor did, which left him room to rely on his sly seductive charms to win women over. Being the middle of the brood that his parents had produced, he was only ever likely to offer a woman a lowly title and a small summer estate in exchange for a marriage contract. Not

11

something that ranked very high among among a proper Lady's list of eligible bachelors. Andrew on the other hand would become the next Lord of Briarden and be able to offer his bride far more prestige and property.

The current Lord of Briarden took great strides to make sure that his sons were well looked after. For each of them who lived to age fifteen, he had an estate sectioned off from his own and a home built upon it to be completed in time for his younger sons to move into them. His message to all of his sons was that family was the most important priority.

Conor did love the company of his brothers, but since he had less to be concerned about in terms of family responsibilities, he did what he enjoyed best. He made a gallant sport of women and socializing as his pastimes until he'd finally been set upon by the concerns of his mother who admonished him to make more serious strides toward starting a family. Considering he had six brothers, three well over ample age to be directed in the same manner, it grated him at first that she had chosen him as a project that required undertaking.

The spiritual pressure of Thomas being selected by Father to join the seminary was likely to have set Mother to the task of putting Conor on a straighter path as well. Father believed that he had enough fortune to go around to entrust one son for the sake of religion and had made the choice to send his youngest down that road, to show his thanks for his healthy stock of sons. He promised to no less love his absent son than the rest and to make considerable contributions to whatever location Thomas chose to worship when he took the vows. Surely large sums of grain, seeds, and animal stock would help all brothers of the cloth and not just Thomas. Conor cringed thinking that if his fate had been different, it could have been him walking the long, lonely path of God. Thomas was too young to realize the future that he had no choice in giving up, but Conor knew full well the pleasures that Thomas would never know. It was not a fate he could fully imagine. Alone-with no warm body to lie beside him on cold nights.

Conor suppressed cringing, refolded his hands in his lap, and leaned his head back against the older, outdated, worn velvet-clad walls behind him. When his mother had proposed meeting with Ms. Guliana Robbinbury several months ago he'd been concerned at the plans being drawn around his neck like a hangman's noose. He balked and made several grand boasts about not bothering to show up to an arranged engagement, though, in the end, Father had taken up his wife's insistent interests and claimed that if Conor didn't meet with her promptly he would see to it to have Conor drugged, brought to a church, and married without so much as a word between the couple. Begrudgingly, he attended the arranged dinner and found that he had actually liked the pretty, plump-faced brunette, and it hadn't been such a waste of time after all.

Minor pain shot down his long legs reminding him of how cramped the carriage quarters were. Quickly shifting his lanky form as discreetly as possible, he tugged at the confining cloth around his groin and legs and rearranged his position while carefully avoiding the fine fabric of Guliana's voluptuous skirt. He took a moment to glance out the window on his side of the carriage and viewed the thick line of bushes that bracketed the field of weeds sprouting on either side of the carriage. Guliana's chaperone, the hook-nosed Ms. Bradel, had exited the carriage earlier when it had come to an abrupt halt in the middle of the field. With a thin crooked finger she warned them both to be on their best behavior while she talked with the driver. The tension between the two of them had increased as soon as the older woman had stepped from the confines of the carriage.

"Why I'll be." He allowed a slight chuckle at his discovery, and he was pleased when her breathtaking gaze was pulled from the window and slid over to him in puzzlement. "I think this path leads right through Lord Somerset's land."

Conor grinned eagerly, enjoying her attention. He leaned forward, coat bunching as he stretched a hand out of the window, and pointed out beyond the row of thick foliage. "Oh, yes," he proclaimed with an easy smile. The Briarden trademark facial dimple caught her attention as she watched him with interest.

"I think it does. Not too far from this spot is where it happened," he built up the suspense as he brought his hand back inside and faced her. "Do you know that a distant relative of Lord Somerset's vanished without a trace, never again to be seen or heard from? It caused a great scandal. Lord Marcus had always been a bit of a distant one from what I've heard, but to leave his young wife with children the way he did broke the poor woman's frail mind. Lord Somerset's young brother, Geoffrey, took over the estate temporarily. Though, once it was determined Lord Marcus was not returning, Geoffrey was declared the new 'Lord' of the Somerset's lands and married Lady Heather and raised the children together."

"It's a cautionary tale for all the children of the area, especially young heirs who would become Lord's. Our governess would tell us the most appalling stories about the disappearance. Of course, we were only small boys at the time. In one version, Lord Marcus was killed in a brutal fashion by highwaymen and left in a bush somewhere, and in another she said he sprouted wings like a bird and flew away. Never to be seen again." Conor flapped his hands extending his fingers and watched as she laughed at his narrative. "She was quite the storyteller."

"Is it true?"

"That he sprouted wings and flew? I do rather doubt it," he joked, purposely misunderstanding her question.

Stray brunette curls bounced around from beneath her hat. "No. That he just disappeared like that."

Conor shrugged and smoothed out his jacket. "It's hard to know for sure really. It was a long time ago and each tale she told was different from the next. It's more probable she was just trying to scare us from wandering too far from home."

"A good trick, I'm sure; considering she had a handful of young energetic boys to look after."

"We were quite a handful," he agreed. "I always wondered why Father didn't employ more than one governess until we were teenagers. Though thinking back on it now, her stories did seem to work until we were older."

"You had an entertaining childhood."

"And yours? Were you always a perfect young woman growing up?"

"I assure you, I was quite an angel. All my brothers and sisters were quite a deal older than I was and most had already gone off to be married, or were close to it by then, so I had no one to lead me astray."

He nodded slowly. Her reply was more formal than he'd been fishing for. He'd yearned to hear her admitting to a pint-sized terror-inducing version of her older self to share in a joke and a smile about the shared information.

Clearing his throat, he glanced back out the window. "Do you suppose our driver and Ms. Bradel have secretly made off without us?" He wiggled his brows at her, which produced another shy smile. She couldn't be too stiff if she could smile at some of his jokes. His true hope was after they were married she might open up a bit more.

Moving to the window, he pushed his head out of the opening and looked toward the front. With his position and the size of the window, he couldn't see beyond the end of the carriage car. It wasn't that he was fatigued from her company, on the contrary—he was actually enjoying a few moments alone with her. He simply had a houseful of eager relatives and guests that were awaiting their arrival for his intended proposal, and he didn't want to be overly late for the occasion. It was supposed to be a surprise. The driver had purposefully taken a longer route so that her family could make arrangements to arrive ahead of them and be in attendance. All that she had been told was that he'd come to personally invite her and Ms. Bradel to tea. Though he was beginning to wonder if she suspected his agenda.

Conor opened his mouth to call out to the front of the carriage when the passenger car jerked forward, throwing him forward. Guliana squeaked as his head slammed on the window frame. Uttering a exclamation of shock, he pushed himself back away from the opening toward his seat. Feeling foolish, he winced as he rubbed the spot furiously, pain radiating throughout his head.

"Are you alright?" Guliana slid to the center of her seat and leaned forward. He might have been more pleased to catch a glimpse of her aiding him if his head wasn't on bloody fire. "Let me see."

Pulling his hands away, she inspected his face. An angry red blotch where he'd struck, and then made the area brighter by rubbing it, stood out from the paleness of his skin. He winced at her prodding but she was relieved there was no blood. "What in the world..."

She was cut off when the horses started screaming like banshees. Whirling around in her seat, she stared at the wall and clasped her mouth, her eyes wide with horror at the sounds outside the carriage. They were truly terrible noises; terrified and in pain, the horses bucked against the confines of their harness and the carriage car was rocked forward and back as if it were riding waves. With no premise about grace or propriety, Guliana crossed the seats squeezing in beside Conor and she wasn't ashamed as she pushed her face into his shoulder. Holding her ears, she tried to block out the maddening high-pitched screams as they were both were thrown around roughly.

"What do we do?" Guliana's voice pushed past her dry lips in a low whisper as her heart hammered rapidly against her ribs. The corset, usually the finest in fashion, was now treating her as if she were a prisoner as it painfully constricted her heightened and terrified condition.

Conor swallowed, still holding his throbbing head with one hand and tightening an arm around her shoulders, pulling her closer. He heard her, though he did not comment right away. If they were animals attacking the horses, surely the horses would have noticed them coming. If they were highwaymen, attacking the horses did not make sense. There was little profit in horse slaughter. His growing concern was the condition of the driver. Usually the men were outfitted with pistols or muskets and

16

swords to help defend the passenger cars, but there hadn't been anything of the sort prior to the attack. No screams of fear from Ms. Bradel either. What had happened to them?

"Stay quiet and hope the horses are all that is wanted from our carriage." He didn't mention how they might get to his estate without horses, and he hoped she didn't bring it up just yet. It would be a long walk, especially in her fine wares.

"Ms. Bradel is out there." Guliana started to move forward but Conor clasped both arms around her tightly, stilling her movements.

"It's best to stay put for now. We can only hope she and our driver is safe like we are. Don't draw attention to us. Don't get near the windows. Don't even look out them or you might be seen." Part of him wondered if he should play a gallant hero and rush out of the carriage to scare off the attackers. It was a grand fantasy, one in which he momentarily played out in his head, though he ruled it out in place of rationality. For one, he didn't know what was out there. Two, he had no true weapons to speak of and the fate of two people were an unknown factor and he couldn't possibly rely on anyone for help if he jumped out and bit off more than he could muster on his own. The idea that something could happen to him and it would leave Guliana defenseless chilled his skin.

He could tell Guliana didn't like the idea, but she didn't try and move again. The carriage stopped rocking abruptly and the chilling horse screams cut off. An eerie silence replaced the chilling sounds of the horse slaughter and Guliana opened her mouth to speak. Conor issued a warning of quiet near her ear and he was relieved when she nodded her understanding.

Something heavy landed on the passenger car. It thumped loudly, writhing against the rooftop making them both jump. Everything shook around them as faint scratching sounds skittered across the rooftop. Pulling an arm carefully away from Guliana's trembling form, he slid a hand down toward the seat and grasped his gentleman's cane near his knee. It was all he had. He prayed it was good enough.

In what he hoped was a surprise move, he pushed away from Guliana and began to rap the cane along all four edges of the window and kicking an area beneath the opening with his boot hoping the noise might scare whatever it was away. The horses had been harnessed and unable to get away. If he made noise through the cabin, the attacker may believe there was a bigger threat inside and move off. Or at least he hoped so. Thwap! Thwap! Thwap! Thwap!

Taking up the idea, Guliana began to beat at the wall at her side with the flat of her hand. When the cane was pulled out of his hand by an unseen force Conor reeled back in shock. That sealed it then. It couldn't be an animal if it had taken the cane away. Guliana stopped mid-motion, her palms beneath her gloves sore and tingling.

He motioned her to stay against the seat and he moved toward the window. Glancing around, he was unable to see anything but green foliage from Guliana's window. His nose wrinkled at the tangy scent of blood—which was so thick in the air it invaded his nostrils leaving his senses reeling. With a harsh jolt, he felt spindly fingers spear through his hair and jerk him up by the roots. Shouting at the searing pain in his scalp he grabbed at the hand trying to pull him up.

Body jerking and moving to help alleviate the pain he grasped at the attacker's wrist. It felt cold to the touch, slick with fresh blood, and bony like an old woman's. The flesh there moved easily beneath Conor's hands like it was too loose. On reflex, the attacker's hand flexed and sharpened nails dug further across his skull as it tittered at him from above, like laughter. He could feel wounds from the fingers cutting his scalp, the sticky wetness of blood trickling from his scalp.

Desperate to end the white-hot pain streaking through his head, Conor's fingers tore into the skin of his attacker trying to break free. His counter measure seemed to have no effect on his still unseen assailant. Indeed, the grip seemed to get tighter. Hot sweat and blood rolled down his face as he braced his knees against the inside of the carriage and pulled, feeling the muscles in his stomach burn in protest of the tug of war.

As he fought with the assault, he felt Guliana wrap her arms around him from behind, chest flush against his back, tugging to try and pull him from the strong grip. He could feel the struggle in her body as she tried to free him, but she just wasn't strong enough to be of much help. He wanted to tell her to keep away from the window, but he wasn't able to get the words out. The last thing he wanted was to put her in any further danger than she already was just by being inside the carriage.

Behind him he heard the carriage door slam open on its hinges. Guliana went still against him and he felt her crane her head to look over her shoulder. Her sharp inhale was followed by a blood-curdling scream aimed at his back. She tried to move forward, wrapping her arms tightly around him, as if her body could meld with his, but her weight was yanked easily away from him. He felt the frantic grip of her fingers slip from around his waist and the warmth on his back replaced by air. He grunted, shoving his tongue out between his teeth, and twisted his lower body to stretch out, to try to hook a leg around her waist. His hope was to hang onto her as best as he could to help pull her back toward him with his legs. But in his precarious position, he proceeded to miss her, instead managing to kick her solidly with his boot instead.

He struggled and swore, choking out her name, listening to her terrified screams and the mad rustle of her dress as the carriage shook behind him. Blood and sweat rolled into his eyes, making them sting. He blinked rapidly to try and remove the offensive combination and that's when he realized that over the din behind him, that he could actually hear the ragged breathing of his attacker above him. Galvanized by this revelation he tried to figure out how to escape and rescue Guliana. His position in the carriage had slipped when he tried to grab for Guliana, and now his shoulders were pressing roughly against the side of the window, his neck stretched tightly.

The scurrying behind him lessened, but Guliana's screams continued and he realized that she'd been dragged from the carriage kicking and shouting for him. Howling with a rage he didn't know he possessed, he bit his bottom lip and pulled on the arm from above. Bruising his bottom lip, he pulled until he saw stars in front of his eyes and the horrible pressure felt like tearing along his scalp. Eyes watering and uttering cries of pain, he continued to pull as the arm above him held, its grip never lessening. What the bloody hell was this thing? It had a vantage point over him being above him, and it was clear that its strength surpassed his own, but it also had stamina to have held on this long without much gain on either end.

Quickly, before he could rethink it, he pulled hard, placed his knees on the carriage wall, then manage to brace the soles of his boots against it. Bending his legs at the knee, he jerked upwards with all his strength. He struck his head on the ceiling with a force that made his head swim. Shaking the feeling out so that he didn't lose consciousness, he felt gratification hearing his attacker issue a loud screeching cry of pain as its cold, pale arm crashed against the frame of the window. Immediately, the hand let go, and Conor fell to the floor between the seats in a heap. Chest heaving and covered in sweat, blood, and his own drool, he stared weakly at the ceiling, grinning in morbid satisfaction as his attacker mewled in pain.

Groaning, he rolled over onto his chest, wiped his face dry on his coat sleeve and pushed himself up onto his knees. His body shook hard, urging him to roll into a ball and rest, but he pushed his fatigue and throbbing wounds aside. Looking out of the open carriage door, he scanned the area.

The compartment shook as a heavy weight leapt from above. His eyes widened in shock as he saw a pale white figure on four legs streak through the tall unkempt grass and disappear through the bushes before he could get the best look at it. He was able to still hear Guliana calling out faintly, and it prompted him to get moving. She was still alive. He crawled to the door and pushed his legs out; boots first. They wobbled when he stood, threatening to buckle as he laid a palm out against the exterior of the carriage to stabilize himself before he fell over.

Unsure what he was stepping out into, he braced for an attack. He dug his fists at his sides and tightened his arms, prepared to use them for whatever attack came. He knew it was likely that he could be cut down where he stood, as defenseless as he was, but he had no choice. Looking and smelling something like a beaten beggar stumbling from a brothel, he lifted his head to stare the threat down.

When none came, he relaxed slightly and had a better look around. The carnage in the area was like something he'd expect from a battlefield. The gore was scattered around the carriage in thick, stringy, wet clumps of blood, manure, and horsetail in every direction as if there'd been a black powder explosion. Unrecognizable chunks of viscera dripped down the carriage exterior, slipping down and hanging from the driver's seat. The stench in the air was sickly sour and thick. Bile rose in his throat and his eyes grew involuntarily wet as his body heaved the contents of his breakfast beside the gore stained carriage wheel.

Collapsed to his knees in the dirt, moisture dripping from the tip of his nose, he lifted his heavy head and caught sight of his cane lying on the ground. Jolted, he darted forward, rushing across the space between the wheels to grasp it. Pushing backwards just as quickly, he jumped to his feet, turned, and began to run. Ignoring the dizziness in his head, his only thought was to find Guliana now. Throat tight with uncertainty, he held the cane like a sword and darted through the long grass towards the thick brush beyond.

Conor had no way of knowing how many there were…or even if he was capable of saving her, but there was not a bone in his body that wouldn't try. He pushed past the bushes quickly, ignoring the sting of leaves slapping his face. Rushing through them, he almost lost his balance and fell forward into the yawning wide hole on the ground. Flailing wildly, he used the cane to regain his balance.

Conor took in the sight but didn't quite understand what he was looking at. Dirt was piled on the side of the hole as if it'd been dug from the underside up. When he caught a flash of cloth and the underside of black boots before they disappeared completely in the hole, his mouth dropped open in shock. Swearing, he looked around. There were four other large holes; wide enough to fit people through them if they crawled, but each impression had been filled with dirt. This one had not.

A rush of anger and adrenaline spiked through his body, and without any thought to his own well being, he dropped to his knees. Thrusting the cane ahead of him, he squeezed into the yawning hole in pursuit of Guliana and the attackers. Utter darkness closed in around him as he moved forward. The tunnel gave off a cold chill that felt oddly relieving to his overheated skin.

Grunting with the effort that it took, he continued to move forward; chasing them down using the tips of his boots, his knees, elbows, and the leverage of his cane to propel him onwards. Mimicking an inchworm, he grasped and pushed as he went along. Energy being depleted, his body gave him little gratitude for the prolonged strain that he was putting himself through.

It wasn't long before the air became thicker as he crawled, becoming difficult to catch his breath the way his lungs demanded. He forced himself focus on the attackers instead of where he was and what he was doing. Whatever these things were, they had presumably made off with three grown adults silently and had slaughtered the horses. They hadn't left whole carcasses behind which meant they must be carrying their bounty. The way he'd seen his tormentor move, on four legs like that, it had a definite subterranean advantage over him despite the burden of dragging what they'd taken.

With a disheartening feeling in his chest, Conor knew he faced another dilemma as he struggled to keep going. He didn't actually know what he was planning to do when he caught up with them. Engage in a tug of war in the tunnel with Guliana's possibly unconscious body? Poke his attacker to death with the tip of his bloody silly cane? The questions and mocking answers swirled at him. All he knew for certain is that he had to catch up. As impractical as his rescue would likely be, that part mattered first. He'd have to figure out the rest later.

Struggling, his muscles screaming, the rich scent of soil filled his nostrils when he took his next breath. Particles floating in the dense air from the previous travelers was now being sucked into his mouth. Clearing his throat, he pressed his head close to his chest to avoid the plume and tried to ignore the multiple aches and pains all over his body.

Conor groaned knowing that if something were to come at him in the tunnel, he'd have no strength to fend it off. Then in an unintentional event of fate, his body simply refused to go any further and he sagged weakly against the dirt floor to rest. Trying to avoid breathing in more dirt, he pulled the shirt beneath his jacket up more fully to cover his mouth. He had no choice other than to stop- at least for a moment, that's what he told himself.

So he rested. Tuning his ears to pick up any sudden sounds of movement around him. There was nothing. No sound at all, save his own bodily noises as he sought to calm his racing heart and give himself a minute to relax. He didn't want to admit defeat, and grew concerned when despair started to creep into his senses. Expelling a large breath, he raised his head and pushed with all his might to resume moving. It took tremendous effort and his arms shook with fatigue but he made himself to push onward.

Dirt sprinkled down as his hair brushed the top of the tunnel. Keeping his eyelids halfway shut, he managed to keep most of the dirt from getting into his eyes. It sprinkled down over his cheeks and clothes as he passed through; molding everywhere his skin was damp. He had to catch up. He felt a cold ache settle in his stomach as he feared for Guliana's safety.

Conor moved blindly that way until suddenly there was no earth beneath him and he fell straight downwards, crashing onto a hard, earthen-packed floor below the tunnel. Losing the small amount of air he'd had in his lungs, he gasped like a beached fish on his back. When he came to his senses, he realized that he was curled up and shivering in a cold place with a dim light radiating from somewhere behind him. Blinking, he turned his head, feeling the sore muscles protest with the movement. His scalp felt as if it was on fire, and a persistent dull ache throbbed unevenly in his head.

Drip, drip. His ears seemed to focus on it in the darkness. Water? It could be, but he couldn't see it and be certain. "Ms. Robbinbury? Are you here?" His voice cracked on the whispered words.

He was getting all too familiar with the pain that shot up his back when he adjusted his position and sat up, but he winced just the same. The air was cool seemed to float on a breeze and lick his sweaty face. He turned his head toward it and noticed a strong, unfamiliar taste in his mouth. Wiping his mouth with the back of his hand, he felt around and discovered the cane lying by his side; he wrapped his fingers around it, glad not to be completely unarmed.

He tried standing, but it felt like the ground beneath him had come alive under his feet and he staggered as his vision spun like a child's toy. Falling to his knees, he gagged when his stomach churned. He quickly decided that standing, for now, was not going to work. But he'd be damned if he couldn't crawl, and with much less discomfort, too. It gave him more of a sense of accomplishment than just lying there crumpled on the ground. So that's what he did.

If he didn't feel the loose dirt against his palms as he shifted forward, he might have thought he was crawling on fine marble. It was so cold. Almost like ice. But when he lifted his shaking hands, they were not wet.

He crawled toward the light, squeezing through a jagged hole he found in the wall, and stopped midway through, legs dangling on the other side. There was some kind of pool in the floor of the earthen chamber. Even though it seemed impossible, it must have connected with a light source from somewhere above ground, because the pool was glowing a soft crystal color. It looked like something out of a dream. He shook his head to make sure the vision didn't disappear. He was satisfied when it didn't.

The sight of the water captivated him and he crawled toward the edge. He hadn't realized it before, but his mouth was dry as the dirt he'd crawled through to get to this point and his mouth exploded with the desire to drink from the source before him.

It wasn't healthy to drink water. From birth he'd been taught that it wasn't clean to drink from. Anyone looking at him in this moment would advise him not to touch the stuff. But then, if they were lying here mesmerized by the tempting sight of something to drink, maybe they would think the same thing he was. With what he'd just been through, water was the least of his worries.

He had to take what he could get. Tucking the trusty cane under his armpit, he fell upon the edge with a grunt bracing his elbows on the edge. Then he cupped and dipped his hands under the surface, scooping some up. He smelled nothing noxious when he sniffed suspiciously, then he tentatively took a sip.

It tasted fine.

Actually, more than fine. He'd never had anything so cold and satisfying in his entire life. The coldness had a stinging sensation to it, smoother than alcohol, without the thick acrid taste that ale provided. It felt completely wonderful as the icy liquid slid down his throat.

He threw his reservations to the wind and, placing the cane beside him, flattened his body out before the gleaming water. He lowered his head to the pool. Slurping at the surface, he drank as much as his body could take and nearly let his head sink when his neck struggled to hold up the weight any longer. When his lips were good and numb, he pushed himself back and rested his forehead near the edge.

If he could manage to hold his breath long enough to explore where the pool of water went, he'd be able to find a way out. The idea went through his mind as he laid there, body aching, energy spent. But he had yet to get a glimpse of Guliana and he couldn't justify leaving her behind after coming so far to find her. He wouldn't be able to forgive himself.

He tucked himself a protective ball, feeling the cold liquid settle in his stomach like stone and spread like cold porridge. He let his mind drift as he lay there in complete exhaustion. The thought of exploring the area for a way out was tempting but he didn't yet have the strength to pull it off. The thought of leaving Guliana behind didn't cross his mind as he lay there squinting at the light under the pool of water.

The corners of his mouth creased, and he closed his eyes as he played back the course of events from the carriage ride. He was only vaguely aware as time passed. It was as though he was in a fog that wasn't lifting. Groggy, his eyes opened and he looked around.

Guliana! His body jerked as he quickly uncurled from his position and sat up blinking. He swore, feeling deeply guilty as he realized that he might have been asleep. Bloody Christ, how long had he lain there beside the pool while she was in danger? His memory was still cloudy, but he remembered visions of blood and the horrifying echo of horses screaming in his ears.

Cursing himself, he struck the ground beside him in shame. Here he was lounging around like he was on a bloody holiday when he had come down here to find her. It was unacceptable. He had to get moving again. He quickly found that getting moving again wasn't easy as his body protested every move that he made. But he made it back to the hole in the wall and looked through. It was still dark on the other side but he didn't hear anything in there.

It had been easier to squeeze into the room that it was to squeeze back through it as jagged pieces of the wall threatened to shred his middle to pieces with one wrong move. Conor moved to avoid the scrapes, curving his back to avoid the sharp surfaces. As he slumped unceremoniously down onto the floor, his intentions, as brave as they were, evaporated in an instant. His stomach began twisting inside him as if it were laundry being rung out. He grasped his midsection, moaning as he writhed on the floor, pushing his face against the cold floor seeking solace as his forehead broke out in a fresh sweat.

Something was grinding his guts, churning through them with devious intent. The sensation was horrendous, and he had sudden trouble controlling his bowels as something burst low in his gut. Urine and watery stool began leaking from him in uncomfortable equal measure, burning and tearing at his delicate orifices as it stained his once fine trousers. He could feel everything spread through the seat of his pants trying to find a way out of the confining material, warm and squishy as he silently begged his body to stop what it was doing. His senses were well past the strength to gag at his own stench, as he lay there mortified at his bodily behavior. Tears leaked from the corners of his eyes in shame as his bowels evacuated. He had never been so sick in his entire life. His entire body was betraying him.

Some time later in his abject misery he grew aware of being watched. Uncomfortable, and still twitching uncontrollably in his own stinky waste, he peeled his fevered eyes open to see a man staring at him. A humiliated blush broke out over his face as he tried to come up with an explanation for his condition. He opened his mouth to speak, but his breath rasped between his lips and he couldn't form words.

With the dim light from the pool shining into the room, pale white skin stood out against the darkness. What…? Picking his head up weakly, Conor's neck protested and shook at the weight as he tried so hard to focus while he had the man in his sights. Conor's vision blurred and he saw less detail than he would have liked, though he finally realized the figure he was looking at was not a man. It was one of the creatures from above ground that had attacked them. What was it? What were its weaknesses? He was unable to hold his head up any longer and sagged back down on the ground feeling drained, but positioning his head to keep it in view.

The thing moved, and Conor stared as best he could while one of his eyes twitched madly in its socket. His mind wanted to take action, but his body would not obey. The pale, skinny, but oddly muscular looking figure was holding something in its hands. Gnawing on something.

A bare arm. A recognizable glove covered hand. Conor's mind screamed as his lips trembled in horror.

The thing that lived under the dirt longer than he had a memory to know otherwise had come into the cold room because he knew that another treat was there. Since it was probably dead from the long fall, he had planned to sup upon it while the others of his kind ate the ones dragged from above. All he had gotten was a scrawny limb, one that had already been mostly picked over and cast aside. When he had chewed through the protective covering, he had found more meat. Not a lot, but some.

He had come through the tunnels quietly, as was in his nature, and was amazed to find the other food seemed to be still alive. This would make things that much more tasty. He sniffed the air, recognizing the foul stench, though not particularly concerned about it. Most things shat themselves before they died. The food was curled on the floor and looked in pain. The creature didn't much care if the food was in pain or not—it was going to die one way or another anyway. Chewing off a bit of meat from the arm, he reached down and absently scratched his flaccid bits that dangled between his legs, careful not to slice himself open with his own nails.

He moved forward watching the writhing food with a keen interest. The glow from the hole in the wall caught his attention and he glanced at it. No one went in there. The cold wet place was no good; a rotten place. They stored food here because it made the most sense to store it close to the cold wet place, because it was nicer to eat cold food than warm rotten food. It was just luck that the invader had landed in one of their storage rooms.

Not entirely mindless, the subterranean species lived underground and stole food to survive. Having been driven there centuries before, they lived mostly unnoticed until they struck out for food. They were not highly intelligent, though they evolved with a sense of community…hunting in packs and looking after each other.

The food on the floor was blubbering some unknown language, but he had no pity or remorse for it. Food was meant to be eaten. It was not his fault that the food was here. But he would reap the benefits of feasting on the food's sweet flesh.

3

"Ms. Robbinbury!" Conor sobbed. "My sweet Guliana. What have you done?" Conor wanted to pick himself up from the floor and kill the vile thing. He wanted to tear its eyes out and squash them between his fingers and then beat it to death with his naked fists in a rage of injustice. His Guliana was dead, eaten by some horrid creatures under the soil. How could it have come to this? He weakly patted the ground around him and realized that he'd forgotten his cane back in the room with the pool. Shouting out at this new misfortune, he knew that he was in no condition to retrieve it—or attempt to fight off his attacker without it for that matter.

He watched as it slunk further into the room, creeping around him like a wild dog, as he lay helpless on the floor. Tears welled and rolled down Conor's cold cheeks, trickling into the dirt below him. He wasn't a man who gave in to tears often but his world was crushed and he faced the realization that his life was coming to an end and had no way to stop what was coming. The emotions swirling inside him were overwhelming. He would not die this way. To be feasted upon in an underground dirt cellar by some thin pale, white bastard of a monster.

Poor Guliana. His heart ached for her, having to have die in such a horrible way. Knowing that she'd been torn apart by these monsters made him grieve deeply in spite of his physical pain. He tried to vomit because the sensation to do so wouldn't be abated. He dry heaved instead, his already spent body bucking and hacking as he rolled in his own mess.

The creature moved forward, slinking along the wall and sniffing at him. It poked his leg beneath his trousers and Conor howled at it, trying to jerk his leg from its reach.

"I'm going to kill you if it's the last thing I ever do in this world," Conor vowed.

He felt the validity of his words in his heart. He never felt more certain of anything else in his life, but even as he felt the conviction of his words, he was not completely sure of his capability to do the deed. Weakly he pushed himself over. He stared at the hole in the wall. If he could make it there, he could swim and get out. He'd go and get his brothers and weapons and wipe the whole bloody place out. Death to them all. He preferred they died slowly, but really any death would do. Invigorated by his need for justice, he began crawling toward it as fat streams of drool rolled from his bottom lip. Oblivious to the drooling problem he grunted, splattering thick drops along the floor with each slow and determined movement. The creature snickered behind him as if something was funny.

Fevered face aflame with anger he continued to drag himself across the floor with his forearms and the toes of his boots. His ears zeroed in on the creature as he picked up the sounds of it following him as he moved. He wasn't surprised when he felt the thing poke at his calves as if to communicate the idea of reaching the pool was just a dream. Everything Conor knew about this type of creature suggested it received tremendous enjoyment from taunting its victims. Victim. The word sounded like he was giving up on himself when it crossed his mind. Maybe he was. Blinking away the eye wetness, he concentrated on the pool entrance.

Unbeknownst to him, his sweat and struggled actions just made the creature more excited at the thought of eating him. Had Conor known, it probably wouldn't have mattered because there wasn't a single thing in which he could do to stop it. His body was burning up and the sweat rolled off him like it was dew from morning's grass. Even as ill as he was, he wasn't going to just lie there on the floor without trying to avoid being eaten alive.

The creature took the opportunity of Conor's struggles to leap onto his back. Conor had expected it, but he hadn't fully expected his own inability to maneuver the attack into something that he could use for himself. He basically lay there in a sweaty, disgusting heap, and let a monster jump onto his back. He took the brunt of the action hard and his breath expelled heavily against the floor and then sucked in dirt. He tried to cough, to dislodge it, but he was having a difficult time with the creature on his back as he half-heaved and gagged pitifully on the floor. A sense of humiliation overtook him. If his brothers could see him now, they'd be so ashamed. He hadn't saved Guliana, and now he couldn't even save his own endangered life. It was only a matter of time now, he knew, before he died. He felt heavy grief in his chest as he realized that his family would never even know what had happened to him.

The creature took Conor's sweat streaked long hair, threading its spindly digits through it and yanked his head back. Stars danced in front of his eyes and he wondered how much more he could take. It leaned over him, its feet digging into the muscles of Conor's buttocks, its knees digging into his back as it bent his spine at an uncomfortable angle. It sniffed Conor's hair and licked a rough tongue along the side of his neck, tasting the salty wetness peppered with dirt as it went. Disgusted, Conor tucked an arm close to his rib cage and drove it back into the creature hoping to hit something good enough to make it lose its grip on him.

The elbow connected with the creature's ribs taking it by complete surprise. It howled and let go of Conor's head, but it continued to thrash up and down on his back, wailing. Mid-leap, Conor pushed up with his arms and dislodged his unwanted passenger. Frantically he pushed his knees up underneath him and scrambled as quickly as he could toward the hole in the wall.

Conor stared frantically at the light beyond the hole; and he might have made it if a deep, gut-wrenching pain hadn't made him scream out in agony and collapse. It was involuntary and there was nothing he could do. Something new inside him seemed to have burst and an intense sizzling burn erupted within his belly feeling as if he'd been stabbed with a hot poker. He could do nothing but weakly sob against the pain and rock himself, his mind, reaching out and trying to urge his body forward, trying to tell himself that he didn't have much further to go. But his body would not listen. It could not. It was fighting an internal battle of its own as another enemy force was stealing his life away from the inside.

The creature, unaware of the torment going on inside its intended feast, rushed at the food on the ground with savage intent. It griped the food by its arms and looked into its odd looking, dirty, wet face.

As Conor stared back, he thought he could recognize humanlike features, but whatever the creature was, it was too far-gone to have been a civilized human being. "You. Are. Not. Going. To. Eat. Me," he vowed, with each word painfully uttered into the face of his attacker.

Beyond thinking of anything but inflicting pain on it, Conor held his breath and forced his face forward and plunged his teeth under the jaw of the creature and began to tear at the flesh there. If Conor was going to die, and his mind told him there was little hope otherwise, he'd choose how. And he intended to take his bastard attacker with him.

Once the creature was dead, Conor would struggle to get to the pool. He knew he wouldn't make it out now. He doubted he'd be able to hold his breath long enough to explore to get out. The burn in his stomach was getting worse, and it felt as though his insides were being churned up in a kitchen for a stew. No, he might not get out of the pool, but he could stick his head in the water and drown rather than wait to be found by another one of these creatures to be eaten like a common stock animal; or be slowly consumed by the liquid fire erupting in his belly.

The creature above him howled in its own pain and shock. Conor held on, tasting a thick substance that his brain told him was blood. The flesh between his lips tasted oddly like cold, uncooked fish, and not a particularly tasty one at that. Greasy and grainy at the same time, it tasted soft and sour in his mouth, and he wanted to gag against it. Regardless, he held on, pulling at the skin and opening his jaws to take more to ravage a bigger hole open. His counterattack became an avenue of revenge as he tore at the creature's neck above him.

Another spasm rocked his body and he felt as though something was now bursting in his chest. Finally, he let go of the creature and fell back shouting as his body jerked. In his chest he could feel his heart struggling to pump. All the sound died out around him, and a buzzing filled his ears as he stared, blinking slowly and urging his heart to continue to keep beating. He saw the bucking creature above him moving in a slow speed as black blood spilled from the hole.

Shrieking above its food, the creature sensed its advantage, but it was having a hard time focusing on it. Lashing out with its sharp fingertips, it caught the flesh of Conor's throat, slicing it into thick ribbons of flesh, spraying blood, and exposing bone.

He'd almost made it. The thought echoed in his mind as his gaze fell on the ceiling. He watched with a dreamlike quality at way the water ripples reflected on the ceiling over the creature's shoulder. The effect was hypnotic to him as his neck was being torn out. He barely even felt the gouges and his blood gush from him. It puddled around him as he choked and gasped, staring up at the patterns that the water made. He could look nowhere else.

Above him, in his own dying panic, the creature dug into the foods chest, finding the rib cage easily and digging in to grasp it. He didn't have the strength to peel the ribs back to gorge at the treats inside like he wanted to; so he raked his sharp fingers through the food's abdomen, spilling open its guts. He did not notice that the insides had somehow burst already, thick with tainted blood draining from the cavity. The creature did not know to think such a thing could have happened. It might have cared if it'd known.

The creature finally fell, weak and dizzy from blood loss and spread out, gasping next to its victim. He stared at the dead face of his own murderer. The glassy eyes of the food would have made a tasty snack if the creature hadn't made a mistake in underestimating the food source. As the creature stared at the mess that had once been Conor, it wondered for a brief moment where the food thought it had been going.

A fever began to burn in the creature just before its own death, though it did not notice. When the cold sweat broke out, it didn't know any difference between sickness or oncoming death. It twitched and found itself captivated by the patterns that the pool made. It had never noticed that before. But then, the pool was forbidden. It was dangerous. No one ever went there. It wasn't a safe place.

PART 2

1

Lock's Landing, outskirts; English countryside, 1804

Something hungry squatted in the bushes and watched the figures as they worked in the dark.

She could smell their sweat, and the thought of bashing their heads in and slurping the runny insides excited her. Her enlarged eyes glittered like black gems in the sparse light and a sticky trail of drool escaped her engorged lips.

Many centuries ago, her kind had been similar to the humans that she was spying on. Hatred, discrimination, and fear had driven their odd ways underground by others who did not understand them. They lived like moles now, finding succulent sustenance in meat from the surface. They were an inbred species, once believing that their blood was the purest. As their numbers dwindled year by year due to lack of females to breed, it became even more usual for females to mate with sons or fathers to reproduce. They could no longer mate with humans if they wanted to. Their sole purpose for inbreeding had been lost to a purpose they could no longer remember as a species. Now, it was just a part of life. Over time they had grown to adapt to all of the conditions that it took to live underground. Slimmer, faster, muscled, though a bit dumber and less able to communicate verbally with each generation.

They were spread out through England's underground in shabby quantities, unbeknownst to the mass groups of humans who traveled so confidently above it. The humans believed they knew every danger to them and could see it coming from a distance. While they pranced around with the most wicked of delectable scents, below their very feet, keen senses stalked them like a herd of wild animals ready for slaughter on a daily basis.

It was regrettable that time had changed so much for her people. A great sadness could be felt among them as they felt the strain of loss and hunger every day. There was a time when the people had been ripe with numbers that would have plundered entire cities into the ground, allowing rivers of blood to soak the topside, but things had begun to change for them. As more of her kind were killed off or became dead shells, they had begun to spread out further and beyond their normal borders. Their hunting was more selective and intermittent because of the relentless invader that always followed close behind them.

Undead abominations that were once were held to the bosom as brethren, now roamed rotten and voraciously starving under the soil. In their tunnels. Through their homes. Scattering the remnants of her people farther and wider apart. Their undead husks lurking within the dark pockets of old dug out hollows waiting and hunting them. Abandoning their homes hadn't been easy and the hard lost battle had cost them many lives.

Her kind did not fear much, but they had learned to avoid the ones that would not die. War had been declared on them, but each passing year, the undead things claimed more pockets in the earth...and more of her kind. Some of her race had broken off from the main group, never to be seen again. Whether they had survived elsewhere or had been killed off, it was not known.

Tonight, the female was not thinking of her kind or the undead creatures beneath the earth. She was single-minded in her purpose.

She scratched an open sore absently, quietly waiting for her moment to strike. Blood and puss ran freely down her arm, largely ignored because it didn't matter to her. She rubbed the hard mound of her belly with a rough palm, careful not to rake her long nails against the tough but vulnerable flesh there. She needed food for the youngling in her stomach. Nothing else mattered.

With as much patience as she could muster, nails kneading the soil, she waited crouched behind a thick cropping of bushes until it was the right time to strike.

It was late. The only night in a solid cluster of days that the skies hadn't opened up and drowned the land with rain. Moonless, with a blanket of darkness above them that blotted out the stars, a pair of naughty opportunists worked quickly, completely unaware that they were being watched by something that plotted to eat them alive.

The backbreaking work had already cost them twenty minutes. One of them glanced up at the sky, blew out a hot stream of air, wiped their sweaty face, and then resumed their work. In their line of employment, it was always best to operate quick and have the cover of night hide their illegal actions. It was even better to be toiling in dry conditions instead of drenched ones, considering that wet rot had begun to nibble persistently at their boots.

The second one looked around to make sure the authorities weren't closing in on them. If they were caught, it meant a hangman's noose. Though, it was fair to say that everything seemed to be a hanging offense these days. It was said that the jailhouses were overflowing and there was hardly room for the criminals in them. The over abundance meant that public hangings were up and were in popular demand. Being jailed was far from anyone's mind. It was hangings in the public market or go home disappointed these days.

Death by dangling from the end of a rope was not a dignified way to go. Children and women alike would watch as sentenced criminals kicked, bucked, and shat their pants in the streets. Laughter could be expected if the mess trickled out the bottom of their pants while they were still alive, struggling against the end of the rope. There were few things more humiliating in the life of a thief than dying by the end of a rope; especially if they'd only knicked some food to survive. No one wanted to die, but times were tough. They reasoned that if there were enough food to go around, they wouldn't have to steal. So in some ways, society made them the criminals. Seemed like a fair way to explain it to themselves.

Neither of these particular thieves wanted to find out about death either, but everyone had a tolerance to which they could take no more. Hunger drove many people to lengths that they didn't think possible of themselves before the deed was done. So the thieving was done in the name of empty bellies and they did what they could to try and escape being caught. The cover of night itself was a far cry from a guarantee, but the faster the work was done under the cover of darkness, the better.

Winded and sore, the two figures pulled dirt loose from the widening hole in the ground. The twin wooden bladed shovels moved quickly and quietly, kicking up dirt and musk into the brisk air. The special blades allowed them to dig through the earth much more quietly than with metal. Moving with practiced haste, they deposited the loose stolen dirt onto the large cloth that was stretched out on the grass ready to catch it.

The work was tough and their bodies ached at the labor involved, but the rewards would justify the means in the end. Wiping a hand over his brow, Brock grunted and sucked in a breath as he felt muscles pull hard in his back, sending rays of pain shooting up to his shoulders. It was to be expected that a lifetime of hard manual labor, dishonest or not, created an avenue for many bodily injuries and it seemed as of late that he was collecting more in the name of getting paid. He cursed under his breath, mouth puckering like a caught fish on a line as he rotated a shoulder trying to stretch out the network of muscles through his back.

"I'm getting old," he moaned, not for the first time.

Age was a funny thing that he didn't understand completely. He couldn't remember a time that his body wasn't weighed down with some kind of burden. It was just the way things were, and he'd been content enough to deal with his lot in life. Not that he'd had much choice. He'd been born to parents who died when he was young and he'd taught himself to survive from an early age. Such was the kind of life many had, though the details changed a bit depending on who did the telling. Lately, it seemed to have caught up with him because he'd begun to notice that it took a lot less time for pains to shove off the way they used to. He wondered when exactly the tide had turned when he hadn't been paying attention. At some point, he'd crossed that invisible line where old age snuck up on him and he hadn't even caught wind of it before it struck.

His companion, a skinny young kid named Ed, sighed and stabbed at the ground while glaring in Brock's direction, determined not to lose pace, but annoyed just the same. "If this is some way of getting me to do all the work so that you can sit back and relax, you can plumb forget it. I'm tired of hearing you bellow like a rutting pig about 'age', truth be told."

"Oh, what do you know about it?" Brock complained making a rude noise. Glaring back, he threw a heavy-handed punch at Ed's shoulder, to which the boy dodged. His cap fell off with the movement revealing his stock of long mousy brown hair that looked black in the night. He shook his head and held up a small fist in mock defiance. Brock snorted and spat on the ground and began to dig once more.

Ed sneered, leaned over, re-fitted the cap, and then resumed digging as well. Brock was always trying to lash out to inflict some kind of physical pain. He was a big man and liked to push his strength around when he wasn't standing around complaining. The only reason Ed put up with the man was because the job couldn't be done fast enough alone, and Brock had been a decent grave robbing partner for going on two years now. They had a history that Ed could trust well enough, and they worked easily together, splitting funds down the middle. Brock wasn't a double-dealing cheat like some men had been before partnering with him. The combination was good enough to make a bond as business partners, just not quite enough to call each other 'friends'.

Certainly, the bond would be null and void and likely a different kind of bond altogether if Brock knew that Ed was actually "Edwina". She didn't think he suspected at all actually. She had lived so long as male that she didn't believe that she had made a mistake, but living a constant secret could make anyone nervous. If she didn't bind her breasts well enough, if she slipped up about her childhood while drinking, if she was injured bad enough to where he'd have to tend to her wounds...

The possibilities were there any time they worked together which caused a good deal of stomach upset until their pairing was over with. In some parts she could get away with being a scrawny teenage boy from nowhere. But there were other parts, like these, where she needed to rely on him for things that she could not do alone. Often his sheer size offered her a good deal of protection. His surly attitude helped that much more.

For all intents and purposes, she was male, but no one else would see it that way if they found out. She could trust no one with the secret. It was too dangerous. Trusting anyone with anything dangerous tended to get people double-crossed and killed. And Ed intended to live to rob another day.

Ed was another casualty of dead parents. She'd lived long enough to have blurry memories of her mother. Unlike Brock, whose parents had died during an attack on his home, her parents died from a fevered disease that had swept through her village. It had taken weeks for them to eventually die, despite Ed's ambitions to try to pull them through it. After that, the streets became her home in a neighboring town and she learned quickly that girls received the short end of the stick, often turning tricks to stay alive.

She decided early on that it was the kind of life that was just not going to do for her. One day she'd packed her meager belongings and left, preferring to settle down in a bigger town where she could blend in better. She studied boys and men and set her task to be able to dress, talk, walk, and live life in a new way that would give her far more freedom. No dirty winks from old men or pinches on the backs of her legs to make her squeal. No future of lying on her back just to make a living, if one could call that living. The only things that she lacked were the parts to prove that she was male, which became a burden to hide, but so far had worked out. She looked young for her age and managed to escape being a young fifteen easily enough. Not that seventeen was all that much older-but a seventeen year old boy would be expected to have some kind of facial hair. Fifteen was easier to pull off. She planned to move on long before the locals, or Brock, caught on to her lack of facial hair dilemma.

Pushing at the dirt, she hauled up a new batch of soil thinking of the new places that she could move on to. Secluded places after a while, most likely. It was just a matter of time before she'd have to face the truth about the improbability of being able to pull off an older man's appearance as she also grew older, but for the time being, this was the best that she could do. She'd come to that problem when it came. She could face anything.

She didn't even really like men. How dirty, underhanded, smelly cheats were able to be dominant in society, she never failed to wonder. Still, to pretend to be one she'd had to become just like them, which she'd probably find ironic if she knew what the word meant.

Ed gave Brock the stink-eye when she caught his sheepish glance in her direction. She knew he was going to start complaining again at any moment. It was a routine lately. "What I know about it is that the more you bust a gut about work, the less you do; ends up being more work for me. That's what I know. Do ya think my arms aren't hurting?"

"You're sure getting uppity to work with. I don't much like it. Don't forget who picks the targets and hauls the cart with the bodies, kid. Without me you'd be spinning your wheels in the mud. Good thing I like you."

"Yeah? You're not bad when you're not bitching either. So, let's get on with the cart hauling then so we both can get paid and can go bugger off for the night," she grumbled, as her shovel struck a wooden barrier.

Brock grunted in relief, instantly forgetting their brief spat. He looked around twice to make sure he didn't see anyone patrolling the grounds. When the coast was clear, they started uncovering the box together. It was one thing to be caught digging in an attempted body theft. It was quite another to be caught hauling the actual body. Nodding to Ed, Brock collected the shovels as she jumped down on the closest end of the coffin. With her weight on it, the opposite end of it popped up exposing the corpse inside. It didn't matter what condition the cadaver was in, the sawbones paid good money as long as there was something left to work with.

She watched as Brock stepped back when the smell of fresh rot wafted up his nose. She smiled, wiping her mouth against her shirt, too, but took more joy watching Brock falter. He missed the gesture entirely as he adjusted the cheap cloth around his face. He gagged, spat on purpose to remove the gnarly taste from his mouth, and then he reached down to grasp the corpse around its cloth-covered feet. "This one should fetch a fine price."

"He does like the fresher ones the best. He better not hold out on us neither. You remind him how we always gets what he asks for from us."

"Yeah, yeah." Tugging on the feet, the body slipped from the coffin easily. He dragged it to the cart as Ed climbed out from the grave. Brock didn't feel like going over how things went with the kid. The sawbones would take anything, but he paid what he wanted to pay. Usually it was the same price, but occasionally it was less depending on the condition, which meant they had to divide a smaller share. Neither of them liked it, but thieves couldn't be too picky or they'd find themselves either not paid for their troubles or out of the next job completely.

Standing close to the pile of dirt, Ed bent and had started to lift the corners of the cloth already when Brock returned from placing the body on the cart. Together they began coaxing the loosened dirt to fall back onto the empty grave. It took effort and they were both sweating like it was midday in the hottest part of summer, but it was quicker and easier to do it this way than removing a dirt pile from a mound of grass. When the dirt covered the coffin again, they patted the dirt down using their shovels to smooth it out. Brock reached over and snatched up Ed's shovel with his, and tossed them into the back of the cart where they fell against the body. Ed collected the cloth from the ground and tossed it in the back as Brock grasped the cart handles and began to lead it away from the scene.

"One more of these tonight and we can afford to eat a good meal and grab a room to stay in for the night. No cattle stall for me tonight. Maybe even pocket a few coins for another day." Brock looked sharply at a clump of bushes that shook on the ground a little ways beyond them. Must be an animal, he thought as he resumed walking.

"That would be nice for a change. My belly is rumbling at the thought of a filling meal. Sometimes, I dream about eating food, wake up, and there isn't anything but cabbage from the farm I just stole it from." Ed had begun to really hate cabbage. Even the smell was starting to make her shudder with disgust.

Brock laughed and nodded his head. "Ach. Cabbage. Nasty stuff. Makes me fart all night."

"What doesn't?" Ed sidestepped the expected hand swat and laughed from the safety of some distance.

"I'll have you know that the cattle don't mind," Brock boasted.

"You really shouldn't talk about your girly friend that way, Brock. Sweet girly Bessie loves you." Ed made kissing noises and smiled as she stared up at the sky above hearing Brock moo and then laugh.

They crested a thick grass-covered hill, and it took a bit of extra effort to get the wheels to get through it. Ed pushed from the back and Brock pulled from the front. Breaking the cart free of the tangled grass around the wheels, they stood against the cart, chests heaving. Sighing, Brock wiped sweat on his dirty shirt and pointed. "The next one is over there. Not too far now. A few days older than the one we have here, but the sawbones doesn't give two shits as long as the bodies show up. They just open 'em up for what's on the inside anyhow."

Ed made a face and was glad that she wasn't there when that kind of thing happened. It sounded far too grisly...even if she did help steal them. Pushing onward toward the new site, she found herself wool-gathering about the meal that she intended to have. Some boiled chicken maybe. And fresh bread and decent ale for once. Her stomach growled loudly and she hoped that Brock hadn't heard it. They might both be hungry but she didn't want to bring it up to talk about. It would just make the hunger pangs worse to keep talking about something they couldn't have yet. Bad enough just to think about food especially at a time like this.

Brock hadn't heard the sound. His hands tightened around the handles of the cart as he tugged, with his mind on other things. He was too busy thinking how much his back was killing him, and he was biting his lip not to say anything more about it.

"What we have here is a criminal act, my friends. Just look at that corpse there. These two are grave robbers. What should we do about this, I wonder?" Came a highly amused voice from behind them.

Completely surprised, the pair spun to watch a group wander close. Five men had managed to come upon them when the clouds had covered the moon above, and they'd obviously been too distracted with their own thoughts. She shook her head, annoyed. How had they let this happen? A stupid mistake like this would get them beaten, robbed, and possibly killed.

"You the law?" She was fuming, and the tone of defiance and outrage didn't have to be faked.

One man laughed like a donkey and slapped another man's back. "Good Christ, no, but we would like to relieve you of your good fortune. We, ourselves, were coming just this way to do the same. Scouted a grave out our very selves, but seeing as you already have one..."

"That's a steaming pile of shit. We got here first and this is our body to sell. We don't plan on sharing." Brock didn't sound tired anymore. In fact his backache vanished at the thought of losing the one body they did have. Brock scanned the men calculating the odds. Five against two, well, one and a half. The kid wasn't a very good fighter. They weren't great odds, but he hoped there weren't more of them, otherwise it'd be a losing fight. They had worked out a routine just in case this happened; and he just hoped the kid remembered and was up to it. It was now or never.

"Ed, do it." Brock braced his body for a fight and dropped the handles of the cart as Ed darted forward. Wanting to protect their meal ticket as well, she gripped the handle of the blade in her pocket, withdrew it, and lashed out. She jabbed it directly into the leg of the closest man, twisted the blade then darted backwards, knife in hand and light on her feet, ready to strike again. The man howled and dropped to the ground holding his wounded leg.

Brock's big, heavy fists connected with one man's face and the sound was satisfying as the man yelled out in surprise and pain. From the sound of it, Brock's fist may have shattered a jaw. Ed knew her role did not end there. There were three more of them. She gathered all the moisture she could in her mouth and spat it at the closest standing man, kicking him in the shin for good measure. "Why, you goddamned little shit!"

Ed spun and was off and running in the opposite direction of the cluster of men. She couldn't afford to wait for retaliation as she sped away. She was too small and more easily overwhelmed in a fight. It was her job to draw the men who felt like giving chase to her childish attacks away from their valuable cargo. Any men who stayed behind Brock would then have to dispatch.

Everything depended on stopping that newly acquired corpse from being taken away from them. They would worry about their second selection later, assuming there was time and they had the energy to retrieve another one after this bunch of horse shit.

She sped through the wet grass, her long legs flying over the ground with grace. If there was one thing she was good at, it was running. God knew, she had to have some way of being able to protect herself. Running away might not be the most heroic sort of tactic, but she never claimed to be a hero; just a poor young kid who stole to eat.

Swearing, she glanced down at her feet in the dark. The poorly made boots were literally shredding as she ran. They just could not bear the quick maneuvering, and she almost tripped as the bottoms began pulling apart from her feet. Jumping over a headstone, she lost the rest of the sole and was now running barefoot. The remainder of the boots clung to her shins, sliding up and down her trousers to the rhythm of her movements.

Her feet were steady and strong as she called out taunts over her shoulder when the adrenaline in her body gave way to glee. "Dirty bugger."

She heard someone trip and the body fell hard on the ground with a loud string of curses filling the air. It wasn't long before she was far enough ahead to pull an about-face in the dark and drop to her pre-planned hiding spot. Crouching down, she made herself small in the dark and forced her lips closed to breath through her nose. Ed knew that she'd had at least two on her tail, but she wasn't sure about the rest. The one she stabbed probably wasn't up for a chase and the man with a busted jaw likely wasn't either. That left a third man that she wasn't sure of.

With luck, he was occupied by either being laid out beside his friends or had picked up the chase on her. Which would mean that Brock should be already on his way to their rendez-vous point with the body. This would leave her pursuers doubling back for their fallen friends and having been out smart-ed.

Heavy feet came thudding through the area and the unex-pected happened. One of the bastards ran right through the clump of bushes that she had hidden behind like a blind ox. The toe of his solid—and still attached—boot kicked her square in the ribs as he tumbled headfirst over her prone body. Air shot from her lungs and she gagged violently, grasping onto the bushes. The man crashed to the ground face first and didn't move.

Of all the damned stupid things. It was something she couldn't have planned. Ed groaned and held her ribs as she tried to remain quiet. Unfortunately, she was unable to be quiet enough; large hands reached and grabbed her around the throat from behind. Squeezing, the hands urged her to stand from her position on the ground. They tightened, feeling like thick bands of iron around her neck as she coughed and bucked trying to escape. Her small body wasn't much good against his bigger one.

"This will teach you for running, you stupid boy. I wish it were daylight so that I could see your puny little red bastard face when I choke the life out of you. When you're dead I'm going to piss in your dead open mouth" he whispered into her ear, and his foul breath rushed down the nape of her neck.

Shivering at his excited tone, she came up with an idea. Once, she'd seen a man go from standing tall to going unconscious and it'd taken three men to hold his body weight up when he'd been completely limp. Holding her breath she imagined that she was made of stone and was sinking into a pond and let her body simply fall toward the ground as dead weight.

Used to the struggle and unprepared for the complete lack of movement, she slipped out of his hold. His hands nearly caught her again when he tried to reach for her, but she quickly stopped her descent, squatted in front of him and lashed out with her bare fists punching him in the crotch. He screamed an unmanly sound as he grabbed for his balls and dropped in bewilderment to his knees. Apparently it was the last move that he'd expected. Lucky for Ed, not so lucky for him.

Gasping and wiping her hands over her throat to erase the feel of his, she walked up to him and pulled her knee up hard under his chin. His teeth clanked together and the force knocked him over sideways. "Bleeding prick sore."

She had a few moments to catch her breath before feet pounded toward their location. Beside her, she heard the ox who'd tripped over her begin to move on the ground. Sucking in her breath and holding it in against the pain coming from her ribs, she forced herself to get moving. Making out some distant light peeking through the darkness, she sped toward it.

She had been following the two humans and was about to strike when more of them arrived. Two of them would be a chore enough with a heavy belly, but the numbers were now stacked too greatly against her. Even a dumb creature could tell when her chances would be slim if they all banded against her.

Slinking off, she felt the bushes brush against her lean alabaster and purple mottled skin and more sores opened. Climbing down into the hole, she pushed at the walls around the tunnel with her feet, effectively covering her tracks as she descended into the earth. Retracing her journey, she felt the ache of hunger in her womb. The little beast in her stomach was so hungry. She'd find food.

Somewhere.

2

Lockette Estate, 1804

Within the flickering light of a thick drooping candle, Lady Esther Lockette worked quickly with quill and ink, manufacturing the right tone of the letters that she was preparing. The fragile light source let off a small amount of heat to warm her face even as the chill of the room nibbled at her fingers. Forging handwriting was a tough task made more difficult by the shudders that ran up her small frame. She glanced at the handwritten note from her husband and continued. *Grab hold of your senses for Heaven's sake*, she thought. Years of educated grace and a well-funded upbringing were lending guidance to her nerves and yet her mental state was in disarray. Glad that she was more or less alone, she let a cold façade take over her features and a steel will begin to bury her fright.

A cold, rainy draft whistled in from the shuttered window across the room sending chills racing across her skin. Taking a deep breath, she pulled the thick shawl more firmly around herself patting herself warmer. Esther glanced over her shoulder to the corner of the room. It was dark there and the light from the candle could not reach, but she knew what was there, watching her with cold, calculating eyes. "You should stop staring at me like that," she commanded bitterly. "It's unnerving." She did not get a reply, nor had she truly expected one. There wasn't much communication between them tonight.

Earlier in the evening before the sun was about to settle in for the night, he'd come home with a bite on his forearm insisting loudly for all the blooming country-side to hear, that while he'd been roaming the grounds around the family crypt something man-sized had attacked and bitten him. Richard had managed to fend the 'man' off and return to the manor to attend to the wound. He'd already planned a hunting party to track it down as soon as dawn broke by the time Esther had met up with him in the hall.

The idea was preposterous, of course. It made no sense for a man to bite another man in the dark. Kill Richard because he was off guard, sure, that was possible. But to actually bite? Why not just use a sword or a musket instead? Much more effective. Biting just didn't make a lick of sense. When she put these questions to her husband, he'd grown impatient with her skepticism and struck her twice for doubting him at his word. Cheek stinging and swallowing her displeasure, she watched his large frame stalk away murmuring threats under his breath. Chalking the whole scenario to his reputably bad temper and bad eyesight in the dimming light, she stayed far from his side to let himself cool his head with a brandy and to bandage his arm.

Esther took her time before adjourning to their bedroom, relaxing in the study with some delicate needlework by the firelight, deep in thought. She had been married to the handsome man when she was a ripe fourteen and had mistakenly believed that his kind words portrayed some kind of fond affection for her. The marriage had been arranged with her family, but Esther had thought that she was getting a good man out of the deal. It turned out that he was quick to temper and drank more heavily than he'd let on in their courtship. She soon realized that she'd been trapped with a rough man and a cold home to call her own. By then it was too late to establish to her husband or the household that she was anything more than a young new wife.

When her eyes began to tire, she put the needlework away and climbed the long stairs to their quarters. Searching the room for him, she found it vacant. When she discovered him in the adjoining writing nook, she wasn't very surprised. The private writing quarters held a long lounge chair that doubled as a bed, a sturdy oak table, writing utensils, a long thin door to the hallway, and a lit candle. Richard liked to be able to attend to private business away from the rest of the staff when his library, where he normally attended affairs, wasn't discreet enough. Esther spotted a fresh quill and open-faced letter on the tabletop. Crossing to the desk intent on extinguishing the candle, she was startled to see Richard standing in the dark corner of the room ungentlemanly passing gas as if she would not notice.

She frowned at his behavior and he seemed to ignore her silent reprimand as he faced the wall grunting softly. The truth was, Richard was more inclined lately to do exactly as he pleased since they were husband and wife. During their courtship he wouldn't have dared squeak so much as a chair in her company, lest she thought he'd passed gas in her presence. Short lived bliss, to be sure.

Esther wrinkled her nose and tried to ignore the sounds he made as she peeked at the surface of the desk. She wasn't in the habit of sneaking a peek of his letters within his presence, although she did look into his affairs as often as possible outside of it, to keep abreast of situations that he would otherwise not discuss with her. She hoped that she could make out a few words while his back was turned.

At first she took the words as a joke at her expense. The letter was addressed to her.

My Dear Wife, I feel frightfully ill. I think that I might hurt you like I hurt that poor kitchen servant before I came to our chambers tonight. My headaches, my stomach churns, and I sweat like a pig. Please call for the Physician right away. Something is not right.

She made an incredulous laugh in her throat and looked up from the shakily written letter. "Are you poking fun at me? I don't find this funny in the slightest." She looked up from the letter and turned to see that he was no longer occupied with the wall. He was staring directly at her with a strange pallor around his face. His eyes were red rimmed with deep bags beneath them. His glassy eyes wasn't reflecting the heat of sexual interest, they were emulating the void look of putting a stranger to labor. What she saw in his gaze was unsettling. He looked at her as if he didn't know her. No warmth, no recognition, just a blank, empty stare following her every movement with rapt attention.

Attempts to get him to speak to her went in vain and she began to take his letter more seriously. Something was indeed wrong with him. She had never seen something like it before. A Physician would surely know. It was within the moments of those realizations when she took a hard seat behind his writing desk and began to draft three letters.

A shuffling noise jerked her to the present as she awkwardly signed his name. So far he had been content to shuffle and bump against the wall passing his gas and keeping a disturbing eye on her. *Concentrate.* She expelled a deep breath making the flame flicker. Bundled nerves in her stomach convulsed as she silently prayed that it did not go out. She did not want to be in the pitch dark. Not with him. Her fingers tightened around the quill and she held her breath, grateful when the flame did not extinguish.

Completing the last letter, she stared at the words for a moment allowing them to dry and having a moment to think. She sent a scathing glance at the corner of the room, daring him to speak up now. He didn't. Hearing his ragged breath made her shiver and she signed this new letter with her own name. Then one by one she rolled them, slipped a band around them, and bound them with a wax seal. Adding the family insignia before the wax cooled, she rose to her feet feeling the confines of her dress push against her ribs.

Despite her nervousness she crossed the expanse of the small room elegantly. Firmly, Esther pulled the thin door open and met eye contact with a waiting servant. She gave him a look full of ice and intended threats. "Lord Lockette wants these to be dispatched immediately. No delay, is that understood?" With a nod, he took them and fled, boots slapping loud against stone.

Shutting and bolting the door, Esther barely glanced in her husband's direction and left the nook quickly. There was no physical door between it and the bedroom, and she couldn't have wished for anything more in the present moment. If Richard became worse or began to display true violence in his sickness she would need to alert the estate staff. It was something she hoped wasn't going to be necessary. If the staff found out how sick he was, then they would realize whatever commands she gave in her husband's name were not as powerful. Richard was three times her age and the servants, while polite as to be expected when he was around, were not so polite when she was left alone. Esther did not know if her age ostracized her, or if it was the love they seemed to bear for Richard's past three wives who'd passed on before her. Either way, these walls did not hold much in the way of affection. If she had known what she was walking into from the start, by now she might have commanded their respect, but it was all that she could do to build herself up from their low expectations, with the tentative threat of her husband backing her words. They seemed to know that they didn't have to abide by her will. Or just didn't care enough to take her seriously on her own.

Esther leaned against the ornate bedpost in the middle of the bedroom. She brushed her fingertips against the red and gold draperies that hung around it while keeping a steady eye on the candle in the den until it extinguished with a plume of smoke. If he turned on her now, pulling all affection from her, she might as well forget having any kind of life within these walls. Standing there, even in the darkness that surrounded him, she could swear she could still feel his penetrating gaze on her.

Molly stepped inside with a swift tap on the door to announce her arrival. A squat older woman, she was almost wider than the doorway that she stepped through. Wearing grey linens and a white cap to keep her grey hair in check, she peeked around the room to locate Esther. Her round head nodded upon finding her quarry.

In normal circumstances a Lady's maid would not be able to get by being an ill-suited match to her Lady. It was required of one to attend, care for, and to respond to every whim the Lady required as she was tasked to do. A true Lady's maid would know her Lady's mind before the Lady herself knew the thoughts were crossing it. It was supposed to be a smooth flowing relationship; one to do with respect as much as duty.

In the Lockette estate however, Molly's under-qualified and numb personality was bought and paid for under Richard's ignorant nose. He simply did not seem to care one way or the other, as long as the staff did not disrespect Esther in a public way. Esther's decision, for lack of choice otherwise, was that it was better to have an aloof maid than a cruel one and learned to keep her complaints—that did nothing but irritate Richard—to herself. Esther speculated that his warm feelings toward his past wives had been utterly spent on them and there had been little left over for her turn. Or maybe he was just prepared for her to die like the others and thought it was unnecessary to become attached to her. He never talked about them, so she did not know. The thought made her cold most nights.

If Molly had been a bit warmer with Esther, she would have picked up on the vibes being thrown out and then gone about finding why things were not right. Molly may have found the issue of particular interest to her personally, though she didn't have a sense about such things. Instead, she hustled in with her big hands fluttering around as she walked and began to help Esther remove her clothes.

"Has there been any issues between Lord Lockette and the kitchen staff today?" Esther had to know. Had Richard truly harmed someone earlier? The idea was less settling that he might have than the reasons for why he had. He took to being sick within a matter of hours and she couldn't shake her nervousness over his condition. It was the look in his eyes that had done it. Perhaps there weren't emotions of love flying around their marriage the way that she'd hoped, but he'd never looked at her that way before. Not even when they'd met for the first time.

Molly paused and looked confused as she replaced the dress in the hanging closet. Closing the doors of the beautiful painted cabinet, she stopped to think about it. Molly had seen the red mark on Lady Esther's cheek but had made no comment. As it was only a red mark, and not a bruise to be covered with the necessary salve, it was none of her business. The girl was too uppity as it was. Served her right. Besides, by morning the redness would be gone and nothing need be done about it tonight. Now, the odd question about the kitchen staff. "No, Lady Lockette, I was not made aware of anything particular." Her tone was flat and uninterested. It was true. She'd been busy with other things most of the day and had not yet stopped into the kitchen. Molly didn't feel even a twinge of regret over the purposeful vagueness.

Esther turned, looking Molly over, and inclined her head as she watched the portly woman withdraw a nightdress and drape it over her thick arm. Esther supposed that if there had been an incident, she probably would have been made aware of it by now. Nodding, Esther turned back around toward the nook to give Molly the advantage of unlacing her corset when her gaze met Richard's blank unblinking stare. He was standing just beyond the borders of bedroom candlelight. Watching. Her heart began to pick up its pace as time stood still.

Esther walked slowly backwards, watching him as he watched her, and when her legs met the bed, she sat down heavily upon it. Molly hadn't seen her employer, Lord Lockette, in the darkness and she clucked her tongue in impatience at the Esther's delay. She gestured for Esther to stand up and turn so that she could complete swapping her from her day clothes into her nightclothes. But Esther wasn't listening to Molly and felt as if she was made of stone as her pulse ticked away in her neck.

Richard staggered forward into the light, and she felt all warmth leave her face. He had been sweating profusely which was evident by the way his pale skin looked waxy and wet. His thick, salt-and-pepper colored hair was matted against his neck and forehead. His shirt was plastered against his skin as if he might have bathed fully clothed. Yellow stains with chunks of food had solidified in the area of his stomach down to his groin where it looked like he'd leaned forward and vomited into his own lap at some point. His eyes were bloodshot and full of a red color like she'd never seen before. Like the whites of his eyes had burst. The looks he had given her earlier had made her nervous. This new look terrified her on a whole new level.

Esther opened her mouth to say something, but the words turned into a gasp when he leapt across the room and flew at an unsuspecting Molly. Molly didn't stand a chance against the assault. Richard grabbed her head and tipped it back hard, knocking the cap onto the floor. Mouth open wide, he leaned forward—moaning an unsettling keening sound—and sunk his teeth into the soft, doughy skin of her neck like it was a piece of ripened fruit. In a moment, Molly's face had gone from rigid with shock to incomprehension to terrible pain as his teeth dug into her. She tried to scream, but between the angle of her neck and the fact that his teeth gouged at her, all she could manage was a gargle. Dropping the nightdress, her hands flailed as she attempted to reach back behind her to push Richard away. Flailing and wheezing, she realized that her arms were too small and she couldn't reach no matter how hard she tried to dislodge him. Her large body shook like a sack of flour as arterial blood spurted forward and sprayed Esther in the chest, splattering the corset.

Esther had never needed to scream for help once she'd reached adulthood and out of habit, she let loose a caterwaul that sounded like a cross between a duck being stepped on and a wild monkey. Mortified by her miserable attempt to call for help, Esther used her booted feet to push herself as far from the carnage as she could, but what she failed to recall in her terror was that the bed did not go on forever. She crashed onto the floor on the other side of the bed, striking headfirst on the throw rug. Dizzy, she scrambled along the floor and pushed herself into a kneeling position to peer back up and over the bed. She prayed that the scene she'd just witnessed was not real. It didn't make sense, and her mind was having trouble believing it.

Everything was the same…but worse. Blood flowed from the wound coating Molly's gown and Richard's face. Where the blood had sprayed and splattered against Esther now dotted and stained the bed linens. There was a scent in the air. A fresh, thick metal smell that made Esther gag.

Molly's neck was a flowing red gash. How Richard managed to keep her upright was anyone's guess. The woman was sagging in his arms as he tore more meat from her body. Most of her neck was already missing—a gaping hole of blood and muscle—down to the shoulder where it disappeared into her gown. He was...feeding on her. It hadn't just been a feral bite. He seemed to be swallowing as well which rolled Esther's stomach.

Molly was gurgling, blood spitting as she still tried to scream, reaching out a hand to Esther across the bed. In a moment of clarity, she knew she had to escape the bedroom or risk the same fate. Richard had been coming for her, she was sure of it. Molly had been in the way and she'd unwittingly saved her life. But in order to keep it, she had to get moving. Esther ducked and scrambled on her hands and knees toward the bedroom door, sliding around a footstool. Her knees bruised beneath her undergarments as they struck the smooth stone, but she couldn't feel the pain yet. Pushing to her feet, her boots struck the stone floor hard and she sent a prayer of thanks that Molly hadn't gotten to remove her boots earlier. Then, she staggered at the sudden realization that her knees were actually in pain and almost fell over.

Righting herself, she ran to the door and pulled it open as she heard Richard start to chase her. She looked over her shoulder to gauge how close he was and she shrieked. He'd dropped Molly's body on the floor to pursue Esther. Molly's body twitched, blood still pumping copiously from her wounds as it spread across the floor in a grisly puddle.

He was close. It would take one leaping grab and she'd be trapped. Grasping at the door, she saw the wet blood and feral expression on his face and she couldn't stop shrieking. He opened his mouth and snarled at her just as Esther managed to swing the door closed when he reached it. Richard hit the other side growling and making loud frustrated cries in his throat. When he began to beat at the door, Esther screamed and jumped back into the middle of the hall, her chest heaving as she tried to catch her breath.

A breeze raced down the hallway, and with a shiver that had to do with the cold as much as fear, she realized that by her standards she was practically naked in public. It was against her upbringing to be seen running scandalously around the estate in her underwear. Her mind was admonishing the necessity, but she had little choice other than to be outside her room in them as she moved from the sounds Richard was making behind the bedroom door. There was no way she could go back inside and politely ask for a dress to wear.

Maybe if she could quietly slip toward the trunk of her seasonal clothes on the bottom floor she could pick out something to be properly dressed in. She crept down the hall, careful not to make a sound that would give her away. But as she reached the stairs, the sound of shrilled screams below in the dark made her change her route. It sounded like it'd come from the main entryway. She turned and ran back down the hallway, passing beautifully carved doorways with gleaming polished handles.

When she came to the end of the hall, she grasped the handle to the last door on the left and darted inside. Sometimes she'd privately use the room after Richard had fallen asleep to be away from him. As long as she returned before he woke, he had never known she snuck out in the night. Her secret room had already been prepared earlier and the tall candle had not expired yet. She snuck away the biggest candles for the room because she never knew when she'd be able to slip out in the night.

With shaking hands she closed the door as quietly as she could despite the desire to slam it shut. Leaning against it, she let her wobbling legs go and she sat down hard. Wood carvings sticking out from the door scraped against the corset and dug into her back, but she didn't care. Even as the position she found herself in made her pant for breath from the tight corset, she sat still.

She stared at her hands in shock. Smears of Molly's blood-stained them, and as if to confirm it was really there, she drew a line in her palm and rubbed it between her finger and thumb. With trembling hands she wiped everything against her stockings. She could not believe what had just happened. It felt as if it should have been a twisted nightmare.

When the corset became unbearably uncomfortable, she pushed to her feet and crossed the room. It was musty and most of the surfaces had a fine layer of dust on them. The room, like all the other unoccupied ones, was on rotation for dusting and airing out. Meant to be a room for a visiting child, it was smaller than most of the other rooms and barely used. Richard didn't care one way or another about the cleaning routine as long as something was available for guests when they arrived. It was something she made sure to pay close attention to if she wanted to go unnoticed using it.

She checked on the candle then went to the shuttered window and pushed it open. Cold air swept inside, and her body broke out in goose bumps as rain blew against her. The floor was two stories up. She could possibly wave for help from the window since it faced the courtyard, but she wasn't quite as sure if she could climb out to get to the ground. It didn't seem like a safe idea. She scanned the darkness trying to find a solution when she heard someone shouting in pain in the shadows outside the manor. Esther strained to see who it was and what was happening, but it was out of sight, so all she heard was the horrible sounds of death.

Listening to the rain, she swallowed hard and knew she needed to come up with a plan if she wanted to survive past the night. The letters from earlier assured her that help would come, though it would take some time for everything to come together and rescuers to begin to show up. And now the danger was different than what she'd described, so she'd have to keep a lookout to warn them when they arrived in order to prevent her rescuers from needed rescuing.

She'd need safety, food, and something to drink. The shelter she might do all right with since the estate had many rooms, far more rooms than people, but the food and drink might prove to

be a problem. She was a Lady and she'd never had to do anything manual to survive before. She'd never had to protect
herself before; but one thing was clear, if there were more of the
people like Richard—and by the sounds of it there were—who
were attacking the others, she'd have to learn to rough it out for
the first time in her life.

3

Ed streaked through the grass like a doe, making long strides, tucking her arms close to her sides. But before long, moving became increasingly more difficult. The constant stabbing sensation in her ribs began to take hold, sapping her energy and leaving her with mounting fatigue. Gasping and trying to control her breath against the audible groans became a sickening repetitious cycle as she wrapped her arms around her torso and forced her legs to keep moving toward the lights. She couldn't let herself get caught after what she'd done. It was one thing to run, it was another to have stabbed, tripped, and sack-punched them. They'd be wild donkey pissed by now.

Her left foot found a deep impression in the ground and she stumbled forward, throwing her arms out wide for impromptu balance. Dirty swearing followed the shriek that plopped out of her mouth, as a hot burst of pain streaked through her side. Cocking her jaw, she bit down hard on her lip to stop making any further sounds as she mentally continued the onslaught. Righting her footing, she pressed forward, this time a little slower. It was probably a close call by the way her ankle protested, but she hadn't twisted anything. So she ran with the bulk of her weight square on her toes. The soles of her feet were not happy but it was that or to stop running and be caught. Not exactly an option.

Sucking in dry shallow breaths, she kept her eyes in front of her and was careful not to look back and lose her footing completely. Trying to take her mind off her current plight, Ed went over the checklist in her mind. Run, hide, wait, meet up with Brock, and split the coin. There were ultimately two places to meet up if they'd been separated. One was outside the sawbones' place and the backup was to meet at the The Slaughtered Goat, a shitty rundown little pub in town. Even the poor had standards. When they were sober.

A loud thud rang out behind her and she smiled. One of her pursuers had found either the same hole that she had or the bitch had a twin. Either way, it was satisfying. Curses filled the air, and her smile widened. The men were just not having a good night. It served them right. She decided she'd wait and have a loud guffaw over everything when she was safe and her ribs didn't hurt quite so much.

Straining to keep her focus in two directions she figured that there was a double threat still on her trail. Taking quick inventory, she slid her hands down her hips and discovered that her dagger was missing from the sheath. Frowning, she replaced her arms around herself. The blade had been in sore need of sharpening and the handle wasn't in the best of conditions but it was better than a loaf of bread in a fistfight. She simply couldn't afford not to have it and would need to retrace her route to find it. Weaponry wasn't easy to come by, let alone cheap. It would have been easier to afford sharpening the blade than she buying a whole new one. Later. She'd go back later, during the daylight. The men on her tail and the darkness gave her little other choice.

Making out the shapes of houses with lit lanterns, she felt a spark of relief. Her lungs were sore from breathing heavily, and her feet felt numb from the pounding they were taking. Reaching the closest home, she ducked around the dark side, far out of the illumination of lit lanterns at the front of several homes. Ed pushed her back against the wood and slid down the exterior, out of breath. She came to rest on her haunches, one hand pressed against her mouth and one at her side while she tried to get more control of her breathing. Her heels sunk into the soil, making deep imprints in the softness beneath her. Craning her neck, she leaned out and around the corner trying to get a glimpse of the men.

Ed watched with lowered lids as two large noisy shapes ran past her hiding spot. Relieved, she sagged against the wood, staring up at the sky. She'd rest a few moments and make her way toward the sawbones' place as soon as she caught her breath and made sure the double thieving bastards chasing her were long gone.

The squatting position was not comfortable, and she attempted to will herself to her feet, but there wasn't a molecule in her body that actually obeyed. If anything, her feet begged to be put out of service. Adjusting herself, she sat on her fanny while her body cooled down. Tucking her knees close to her chest, she winced as she pushed experimentally against her sore ribs. As far as she could tell, they were bruised badly but not broken, despite that they hurt like hell.

Leaning her head back against the wood, she watched as the moon began to peep from behind its blanket. She realized, from the corner of her vision field, that someone was standing not far from her. They were standing stock-still, holding something in their arms, and watching her without a sound.

She held out a hand palm out, "I—" but her words were cut off as a powerful blow to the side of her head cut her off. Sharp pain exploded in her head, a white flash formed before her eyes, and her body decided enough was enough, as she blacked out.

It was some time later before Ed was able to pull out of the fog. When she managed to peel her eyelids open, her head felt terrible. She felt as if her skull was split open like a ripe melon at a fruit stand in the market. Her vision blurred and doubled when she tried to look through her lashes to see where she was. Pains shot down her neck to her shoulders as she tried to move and she couldn't help the sounds that she made. She'd been hit with something. A log? She'd been hit pretty good from the feel of it. What day was it? Ed tried to sit up to get a better look around, but felt as if she'd be sick as the room spun around in front of her. She fell back, useless and weak, in a sweaty heap on something smelly and soft, then blacked out again.

The next time she woke, Ed immediately leaned over and threw up over the side of the bed that she was resting on. As her hair hung down freely around her face, she stared at the pathetic puddle and she wondered where the chunks of potato and carrot had come from. Pushing herself back onto the bed, she stared pulled the ceiling into a hazy focus. Where was she?

"Yer up then." A creak in the floorboards rung in her ears as an old woman came into view, standing over her. It was a jarring sight to see a deeply wrinkled, toothless woman's face above her; all brown gums and thick puckered lips as she smiled. Ed swiped out with her hand to ward off the old woman and missed—her aim off target considerably due to her disorienta-tion. The woman laughed and went out of view. "Lost yer supper then? Not that I blame ya. It's not that great. No meat to speak of. Mostly just what comes out of the ground mixed with what-ever I have around the place." Ed closed her eyes and listened to the sounds of the old woman cleaning up her sickly mess.

Ed mumbled some words; she meant to ask where she was, but the words didn't make any sense to her own ears. Somehow, the old woman knew what she was trying to say. "Well, I clocked ya when I saw ya sneaking 'round my house. Old wom-an alone these days isn't a good position to be in when some people are going missing around these parts."

As she talked, unintentional globs of spit speckled Ed's bare arm. The woman talked with quite a lot of mouth noise that some other people might have trouble understanding, but Ed had her fair experience with toothless people so she understood fairly well. It wasn't uncommon for people to go missing, even to get dead...happened all the time. It wasn't really any of her concern. Though it explained the head bashing she'd received.

"I reckon that I shook something loose in that head of yers because ya been out of it for a while. Ya should have seen yer face. All puffed up and purple like I ain't never seen before. Thought mebbe I kilt ya, but ya kept hanging on, so I took care of ya since I don't want no dead body hanging ova my head."

Ed frowned, reaching up to feel her face. There wasn't as much pain as she expected, but she could feel where her cheek and eye was thick and swollen. "Yer face isn't back to normal, no how, but it will be soon. It sure is better than it was. Nothing was broke neither, just swollen like bees were atcha. Took care of them ribs, too." Startled, Ed pressed her hand to her ribs.

"Ach. Didn't know youze no woman until I checked on how come youze so bent on coddling yer side. I seen ya crouched there and thought youze the one causing all the trouble 'round here, so I clocked ya good and solid. Felt bad after I realized youze a woman."

Ed tried to push herself away from the old woman and her flying spit, but she didn't manage to get far. She started to peel off the smelly thin blanket and realized she was naked as the day she was born. Puffing her mouth, she glared at the old woman and forced herself to speak. "You like naked gals, you old coot?" Her words came out like she was out of breath, wheezy and quiet.

The old woman hacked like a cat with a lungful of fur and spat onto the filthy floor. "I'ze checking ya for wounds, girl. Like I been saying, didn't know youze no woman until the clothes came off. Expected to see a shriveled man's cock, but no, seen a fur patch and cloth swaddled teats instead."

Weakly Ed grunted and tried to sit up. Less things spun than before, which she took to mean there was some progress in her condition. "Clothes."

"Yer in no good shape to get outta bed. Stay put and I'll bring ya some stew. It'll help cure what ails ya."

"What 'ails' me is the rutting bloody kick to my ribs and then my head got split open."

"Ach. Not split open, just banged up."

Ed made a noise in her throat and finally managed to get in a sitting position, then looked around carefully. The place wasn't big. Had two rooms with all manner of strips of cloth and clothes hanging from pegs from the ceiling. Rope held up rusted out pots and worn pans. There were no table or chairs to speak of. It seemed like Ed's was the only place to lie down on. A clump of orange carrots, potatoes, and green cabbage freckled with brown spots lay in a heap on the floor in a corner.

The old woman stood upright from a small stew pot in the other open room carrying a wooden bowl at a slant. "Here, eat this. Watch this side though, there's a crack in it, might spill out."

Ed looked in the bowl before accepting it. It looked harmless enough, but it smelled like old socks and cabbage. She wanted to reject the meal, but tentatively, she took a sip of the broth. Her nose wrinkled at the bitter taste; only, her stomach growled for food, so she began to drink it down. The clumps of vegetables in the stew were cut very small and were easy to swallow. When she was finished and her stomach gurgled, which she wasn't sure was a good sign or a bad one, she repeated her earlier demand. "Clothes."

It was difficult to determine which of the dangling pieces of clothing hanging from the ceiling were hers. Everything was the color of coal, oat sacks, and mud. The old woman shook her head, "Yer not ready yet."

Ed groaned, rotating her head carefully. What was to stop her from getting up and leaving? She couldn't exactly prance outside naked, but she sure could steal some of these clothes to aid her in her travels instead. Certainly didn't plan on staying. Let the ancient hag keep Ed's filthy, old tattered clothes. She just needed to find her binding cloth to truss her breasts down. Any bigger than they were and it'd be near an impossible task to be done.

"When did I get here?"

"This here be the fourth day."

Ed groaned and set her head in her hands. Four days? What would Brock have done by now? Would he have assumed she was dead and spent all the coin already? They had never planned on being separated past a few hours. 'Days' was a whole new territory.

Ed tried to scoot to the edge of the bed, but the old woman stepped close and pushed her backwards. "Yer not going anywhere, Missy."

"To hell I'm not. You didn't want a dead body on your hand, fine. I'm not dead. I'm up and I need to leave." The thought that this old woman new her true gender made her hair want to stand on end. She had to get out of this place.

The old woman shook her head and pointed a bony finger and Ed stared at it as it came closer to her nose. "Yer going to wait here for my boy, Hascom."

"You have a cork loose if you think I'm waiting around for any kin of yours."

"I took care of ya and ya owe me. My boy needs a wife. Yer here, yer a woman, yer staying."

Ed had a sinking feeling in the pit of her stomach. She stared, shocked at the old woman, who clearly had a very different agenda than what she'd originally professed, for keeping Ed alive. "To hell with that."

Ed shot forward, all of her focus bent on leaving as quickly as possible. Her head swam like a tidal wave, which didn't help her efforts of escape, but with the threat of her freedom at stake, she refused to pass out. She slammed into the old woman with a jarring force and smelly the blanket fell between them. Ed pushed the old woman's face away from hers, feeling the flabby skin stretch and move under her palms like wet clay. Hissing, the old woman lashed out with bony fingers and grabbed a handful of breast and twisted hard.

Shouting, Ed pulled her hands back and balled them into fists. She quickly brought her arms up, striking the old woman in the head above the ears while bringing up her bare knee into the old woman's' soft belly, forcing her away. The old woman gasped and began falling backwards with her arms pin-wheeling wildly around her. Her feet struck something on the floor and she tripped, landing on the vegetables. Her head landed, bouncing on the cabbage, which exploded in a flurry of green and white, indicating that it'd been quite softer than it had looked. Her thin skirt fell around her knobby knees exposing years of skin that was no longer firm and supple, but thickly veined, saggy, and pale.

Cryptic

Ed looked down at the old woman, "It didn't have to come to a fight, but you couldn't just let me leave, could you? Tell your bastard of a son to find his own goddamn wife." Ed tried to press down the rising hysteria in her chest as her heart thumped madly. Wife, bah! More like 'slave'. This was too close! Fighting nausea, Ed rubbed a palm over her newly wounded breast, then whirled in place and began grabbing clothes down from the hooks. She found the chest-binding cloth in a corner and brought it around her body and wrapped tight until her chest was flat. She slipped the end down in the snug confines beneath her armpit before slipping on a stolen tan shirt. Keeping a keen eye on the elderly matchmaker, she grabbed three pairs of trousers, throwing the discards on the floor, until she found a brown pair that fit well enough to wear. Ones not too big or too small. Admiring a long but filthy, grass stained patchwork coat, she grabbed it and slung it over her shoulder. Finding her own cap, she placed it on her head and shoved her newly socked feet into long brown boots that were too big. Sure, they might be loose, but they seemed like they were of better quality and condition than the ones she had before. Hopefully these would last if she had to run in them. Time would tell.

She looked over her shoulder making a disgusted noise in the direction of where the old woman lay groaning trying to get to her knees. She wasn't very successful, but she was trying. At least the woman wasn't dead. Ed had stolen plenty of things before, but had never had to kill anyone. She was glad it hadn't come to needing to make the decision. It'd be a damn good idea to make sure she never came back around this little shack cluster ever again though.

Pushing her arms through the sleeves of the coat, Ed felt slightly comforted by its ability to hide her skinny form. This kind of event was exactly what happened when people thought they could overpower her, knowing she was a woman. There was just a different level of menace when people knew she was female instead of male. They tried to turn her into something she wasn't. Something she never wanted to be: a girl. To Hell with them all. She was better off when everyone thought she was a boy. She may not be able to fight well, but when it came to her survival, her instincts kicked in to save her. She could hardly ask for more than that.

"Good for nothing old hag."

Ed flexed her shoulders as she moved toward the door. She needed to find her partner. There was no more time to stand around mulling over this unfortunate set of events. As it was, when she caught up with Brock she'd need to arrange a slightly different story for the telling. "I have to be somewhere. Thanks for the knot on my head, stripping me naked, making me puke, and the teat twisting. On second thought- I hope you rot in Hell, you old hag."

4

The creature halted within the old tunnel cocking her head, tensing her muscles, and listening. When the dead things came, they always made enough noise that gave them away; dragging and moaning sounds as if they didn't care someone knew they were coming. Not silent like her kind.

She thought she had heard something ahead of her, but she'd been making too much of her own noise soothing her hungry belly to be sure. She dropped into a crouch, protecting the mound that comprised her middle by pushing it firmly between her thighs. She extended her fingers, spreading them in a curled fashion, prepared for a fight. It occurred to her, that her clan did not know where she was; and she could not call for help without giving herself away to the dead thing. Once they knew a victim was close, they didn't let up. It was maybe the one trait that she admired about them.

When it crawled into the tunnel, she knew why she hadn't figured out it was coming much earlier. The dead thing was pulling itself along—mouth agape—with its hands and elbows in the dark. Its lower body was missing. It was an older thing, and it was possible it had been one of her kind with its withered skin mostly missing in clumps. It was hard to tell.

She looked around her and contemplated her means of escape, backtracking being the forethought in her mind. She could return the way she'd come. The path split a long ways back, but it would mean being far out of the place that she wanted to go. Going forward in the tunnel would take her to a place where she could surface to find the four legged things that roamed topside. They were much easier to kill without danger to her condition since they didn't group up in a defensive attack. She could steal one or two and fill the ache.

She mewled softly in indecision...looking beyond the crawling dead thing to where she wanted to go. She desperately wanted to continue forward, not backwards, but it had its risks. Namely, she could get infected and both her and the beast inside her could wake up dead.

The dead thing hadn't seemed to notice her. It was unknown how well they could see in the dark. Her vision was perfect in these conditions, and in her mind, she mapped out a route that might let her pass the dead thing without attracting attention. Her body demanded basic satisfaction and had waited long enough for it. She was fully against going back and around to avoid it.

She proceeded carefully moving without noise, hands drawn to attack if the need arose. She alternated between taking a step and stopping; waiting, then moving forward again. The maternal part of her was frightened at this idea, but the hunter part pushed her forward believing with some high degree of certainty that the plan would work. Even though she was alive, the smell of her own body was not as temptingly noticeable as a human's; and if she made no sound, she might be well on her way to the feast she planned on.

She held her breath in an attempt to block out its odor. It may have been dead a long while, but the smell of the dead was wholly undesirable to her kind—worse yet if it was a fresh one. As she got closer to it, she stopped as it continued to crawl toward her. She let it get close, breathing shallowly as the musk of it unfurled around her.

As it crawled near her, she carefully placed her feet out of the path of its body, stepping cautiously around it as it moved slowly beneath her. All it would take was for it to realize she was there and it could mean her death. She waited and watched. It crawled pitifully, moaning deep with a sucking dry sound that she could not identify followed by the dragging of its body.

Without a thought as to what she was doing, her long nails skewered the dead thing in the back. Stunned at herself for what she had done, she could no longer stop herself from being in the fight that she'd initiated. She didn't know why she'd done it. Some deep down aversion to what it was, maybe.

Snarling, the dead thing flipped over growling at her, its arms flailing as the teeth sought her skin. The move withdrew her claws from it and she squealed and moved back, swiping out with her fingers. A thicker, putrid smell filled the tunnel as her claws cut into dead flesh and the smell made her choke, gasping for breath through her mouth instead.

The dead thing hooked onto her legs with its cold hands trying to bring her clammy leg to its mouth. It was crying out at her like she was the first meal it had seen in a long time. The desperate sounds made her shiver because they were much like the ones her own body made.

She kicked at it, clawing at the arms until bone was exposed. Chunks of rotted flesh fell from the bone in fatty clumps as she shred through it. But the dead thing did not stop. It lashed out at her with its fingers working on dragging her closer for a taste of her leg. Some blisters broke and oozed while the dead thing seemed to moan in delight at the fresh smell, lapping up the fluid as it spurted out from her leg. She cried out at the fire that erupted as the blisters popped.

Wrapping a protective arm around her swollen belly, the female snarled at the dead thing and began stomping on its head even as it still tried to feast on her. Bone fragmented beneath her feet, shards pushing into the hardened skin of her heel as she continued to strike. Her protective instinct to save the beast inside her unleashed a fury within her and before long the dead thing below her stopped moving.

Heart hammering from the exertion, the female picked up her mangled foot and stared at the dead thing. Was it a trick? She jabbed at it with her good foot and it didn't move. The pulpy remains of its head was soaking into the dirt, forming a putrid pile. Cocking her head, she nudged it again but this time with a long nail.

It took some time to realize that she'd put a stop to the dead thing for good. Then relief and satisfaction coursed through her. Grunting and gyrating to her own beat she made a circle around the dead thing in the tunnel celebrating her joy. She ignored her stinging feet as she released her urine and cackled in the darkness with delight.

She must get back to her clan soon and tell them what she'd discovered. Surely one of her kind had stopped a dead thing before, but she did not know of it. Usually the dead things won out merely because they would not die. This time…she had lived and it had died. There were no words in her mind that described the glory that she felt. For a moment, in a dreary life of one who dwelled underground and hunted to live, today was a very good day.

Suppressing her joyous victory she stopped to listen. No other sounds echoed from the tunnel, but she took a moment to let the quiet wash over her. She'd gotten lucky. Sometimes there was more than one of them and she hadn't paid attention. She couldn't wait to let the clan know what she'd discovered. Squash heads!

Limping and holding an arm over her growling belly, she moved forward hissing at the truly dead thing in a heap on the dirt tunnel. Now that the danger had passed, her young told her that it did not want to wait any longer.

Yes, she would need to tell her clan what happened. But first, she needed to find food. A picture of the four legged animal came to her mind and she smiled a vile toothy smile and moved forward. Ever so gently.

Ed broke away from the small cluster of homes, pulling her soggy cap closer to shield her face as the rain fell. She didn't want to waste time getting to Brock, but she remembered through the haze in her head that she had a missing dagger. It was possible that she might have forgotten about losing it given her state of mind, but when she was dressing she'd patted her hips instinctively for dagger pockets.

Craters of water gathered in mud slicked pools making the trip back to the cemetery slippery. Reaching the far edge of it, she went about trying to retrace her steps as best as she could remember from four nights ago, slipping in the oversized boots along the way. They turned out to be about two sizes too large, and despite skidding around in them, she couldn't complain about the coverage. The material didn't let a drop of water into them which was a large improvement over the last pair of stiff, cloth ones. The socks, although they were dirty—she could feel loose dirt sliding around in them—kept the boots from rubbing too badly against her feet. Ed figured she'd likely still have some walking sores later until she broke them in, but it was nothing she hadn't seen before…just likely less painful with the socks to act as a buffer.

The clothes probably belonged to the old woman's son that she was so fond of that she'd stooped to kidnapping Ed to give her to him. A shudder raced down her spine when she thought of it. If she hadn't woken up when she did, what would she have woken up to later? If she'd been tied to the bed she might not have had the strength to break free. The subsequent thoughts of her fate passed through her mind.

Guilt wasn't a factor in the grand inner workings of her emotions. Everything that she owned was gone, taken or lost with the events in the last days and replacements were needed. There was nothing more basic than that. Luckily, nothing she wore was of great concern to her beyond the cap that she favored and essential binding cloth, both of which she was happy to have recovered. It wasn't her fault that the old woman had popped her on the head, stripped her buck naked, and then stole her clothes. Some women actually got paid for that kind of thing. The being naked part anyway. Who knew what other sick things happened in a whorehouse?

A drop of rain rolled down the bulging collar of the coat and Ed pulled it around closer to her skin. It smelled like wet grass and muddy leaves, which wasn't a horrible combination given the other smells that she was used to. Reaching inside the coat, she had also found a nice surprise in an inner pocket. A few cheap coins. It wouldn't buy much of anything, though finding money anytime was better than having none. She'd be able to combine it with her share when she met up with Brock. Assuming her partner in thievery hadn't spent it all thinking Ed was dead in a ditch somewhere. Ed shivered, blaming it on the weather. Had he come looking for her when she hadn't shown up? It was a prominent question that she planned on asking first thing.

The graveyard in the light of day was less creepy but no less gloomy in the rain. It looked miserable as puddles filled man-made and natural nooks, holes, footprints, and valleys alike. Making a wide sweep of the grassy area where they'd been, she took special notice of the deep impressions where the cart, Brock, and the men looking to rob them had been. Most of the tracks were submerged in water, but it wasn't difficult to make out the thin wheel tracks. The cart had moved off in the direction of the sawbones place and it looked like the pack had dispersed as hoped after she'd taken off, making various deep impressions in the ground.

Wandering much more carefully than she'd done on the nights past, Ed found the bush she'd hidden behind. She almost laughed at the crushed way it looked. There was no mistaking that someone had run right through it. The thing was a mangled mess of leaves and thin broken limbs, divided almost exactly in two parts. Too bad she'd been on the receiving end of the kick. Rubbing her side through the coat, she was glad that it was feeling better than the first night she'd received it.

Ed still grunted as she kneeled to search beneath the misshapen foliage with her fingertips. Her head throbbed, protesting at her prostrated angle. Sucking in a deep breath, she kept looking. It had to be here. It was the only place left. She didn't want to think about whether someone had found it lying on the ground and taken it.

Moving her position to the right, she patted her hand against the soggy mud until she felt something hard under the bush and pulled it free so that she could look at it. Releasing her held breath, she closed her eyes for a moment issuing a sigh of relief then slipped the muddy dagger into the coat pocket and climbed to her feet.

Ed set off in the direction of Lock's Landing, clomping foolishly in the oversized boots, to track Brock down feeling as though for the first time since she stepped from the old woman's house that she might be getting back on an even keel. Occasionally she would scan the area around her to make sure she wasn't being followed. The incident with that woman had left her jumpy, and she didn't want to come face to face with more trouble.

The big knot on her head throbbed under the protection of her cap and the headache felt like it was fit to pushing her brain out of her eyes, but she kept on. At times, she stopped and tipped her swollen face up to the rain to feel the cold droplets against her flushed face. She hated rain, but today it felt good in the way that it always did after she escaped with her life after a sound beating. It happened more often than she would like. The drops felt good against her heated skin, making her forget for a few moments that this time her head had almost been cracked open like an egg.

Thinking of eggs, her stomach growled. Apparently the dirty sock and cabbage garbage flavored stew she'd eaten earlier hadn't held her appetite for long. Go figure. If her luck was extremely good, maybe Brock was still waiting around for her to show up and she could afford to get some real food.

Of course, there was only one way to find out. Even if it was to assure him that yes she was actually alive. They'd never been in a situation like this before. If he thought she was dead then there was no telling what he'd done in the four days that she hadn't shown up. She almost couldn't be sure that she could blame him if he'd moved on, but she had to know for sure. The poor didn't just leave loose money ends lying around if there was something to be done about it. Ed certainly wasn't about to start now.

Gaining on the sawbones' place of business, she recognized the dull sign that held the words "Carver's" with an engraved picture of a surgical saw on it since most people couldn't read in the area. There was no mistaking what the sign was for no matter what people could or couldn't read. Just below it hung a swinging wooden placard with tall letters written on it that she couldn't understand. Though, looking at the boarded up place she could hazard a guess as to what the extra signage implied: Closed and out of town. Shoulders sagging, she approached the door.

"No, no, no," she muttered. Then just to try it anyway, she leaned in under the wooden awning, head out of the rain for a moment, and pounded on the door with a balled fist. Carver didn't keep regular hours like some folks did, he could mostly be found at nighttime, taking body orders. "Come on, ya bugger, open up."

"He ain't in."

Ed spun to view the owner of the frail voice. He was a short, sickly looking boy of about ten, pale around the face, with more white than color in his eyes. Even his freckles were pale against his face when usually a redhead's freckles were sprinkled around like thick gold flakes. His clothes were soggy, and he coughed into his fist as she looked him over.

She kept her distance. Not because he was sickly. It seemed everyone was always sick with something. You couldn't bump into someone who didn't look sickly with all the constant rain. No, she kept her distance because she didn't trust him not to try and empty her pockets. No matter what little she had in them, the contents were still hers. He had come from the corner of the exterior of the house, where the awning was a bit thicker there. A large dry barrel stood beneath it, presumably from where he'd come from.

"Do you know when he's going to be back?"

"Day after next at the earliest. You missed him by half a day. He wanted me to watch his place for him in case one of you 'body' guys showed up. You have one? Can I see it?" His excitement raised a fresh batch of coughing. Ed grunted and shook her head.

"Rats," he muttered, looking truly saddened. He tipped his eyes up to get a good look at her. "You here to take an order then or something? He didn't give me no list to give out."

Again, she shook her head. "Was looking for someone. You know if a guy named Brock stopped by with one a couple of days ago?"

The boy rubbed his earlobe and made a noise in his throat and flipped his hand toward the door. "Big burly guy? With a hand cart?" Then, he rolled his pale eyes up into his head and clucked his tongue. "Sure, I remember the sawbones complaining that some big guy needed to start bringing more of them. Something like that."

Ed nodded. At least she knew that he had made it here. There'd be no reason to hold a dead body until she showed up. Too much risk and the body wouldn't be as fresh. "He get paid?"

The boy made a face and gestured with his hands. "How do I know, man? I'm just a squirt."

Ed smiled and shrugged at the boy's aggrieved tone. "Thanks, kid."

"You want me to tell him you stopped by?" He jerked a small thumb toward the door. Her gaze followed the motion and then darted back to the boy.

"It's alright. I'm sure me 'n Brock will be back with a cart full the day he's back. No need." At least, that's what she hoped would happen. She'd have to find him first and figure out if he had a new plan yet.

"All right, then. Try to stay dry now." The boy grimaced at the rain as some wind blew drops into his face. Shivering, he wrapped his soggy arms around his waist and went to the barrel. She was right. It's where he perched, waiting for visitors.

Ed grunted and wiped off her cold wet face. Staying dry was a huge joke. Not many people could stay dry in this weather. You had to stay indoors or have one of those fancy carriages with tops on them and people from around here, didn't have those.

Cold, wet, and hungry Ed walked the muddy streets to find the tavern.

5

Ed sat in a wet miserable heap in a quiet, darkly shaded corner of the The Slaughtered Lamb tavern glancing up at the straw-thatched roof in skepticism. It looked about ready to cave in. The good part would be, it wouldn't be a heavy cave in. The bad thing would be, there would be no solace from the driving rain.

Lanterns lit and table candles burning, it was easy to see that some parts of the roof had grown water logged with the weight and the relentless wetness and had caused it to start leaking. Puddles had already begun to form along the hard-packed earthen floor.

No one else seemed to mind since it wasn't out of the normal for the place. Most of the men in Lock's Landing tended their regular business in the pouring rain because, if they didn't, nothing would ever get done. The patrons today steered clear of the dripping mess often by moving tables or chairs out of the way of the soft spots in the roof, making due with what they had. It was easier to move out of the drips than to complain about something they couldn't change. Ed saw the brown stain form above her own table and when it bulged and dripped, it hit the tabletop and rolled off the uneven side, toward the floor. Such was the form of entertainment for a while. Duck the puddles.

Not far away she spotted a heavy-chested barmaid with a thick waist and beefy hands that was sporting not one but two hairy chin moles. To Ed, she looked more like a man in a dress, than a woman, which was amusing, given her set of circumstances. The barmaid was entertaining some sparse patrons by standing under a leaking spot letting the water drip into the bodice of her homespun dress. Through the lusty jeers thrown in her direction, seemingly interested men nodded drunken approval by ordering further rounds. Ed may not have been the smartest person around, but she wondered if the joke lay in the ugly woman's achievement to score coin or that it probably didn't actually matter who was standing under the dripping leaking roof on a day like this. The men were there to spend money to get drunk anyway. Rain had a habit of stopping outdoor work early.

The Slaughtered Lamb catered to the hard working, sopping wet, and often overworked men from the fields surrounding the town. The only alcohol serving enterprise for a full day's ride in any direction, it made for a dock in a dry harbor that no man dared to complain about within hearing range of the owner. There was nowhere else to go.

The 'inn' portion to the tavern consisted of a few rooms that had been built onto the back of the tavern for the drunks who passed out there. They were nothing more than open rooms with hay strewn about the floor to spread out on. Surprisingly, those floors saw more action than seemed possible. There'd been times Ed herself had found been there, with nowhere else to go. A hay perfumed room and leaky roof was better than none when the rain just didn't stop falling and when she had the coin required to collapse there in a heap. She didn't have to enjoy the décor- it was just a place to be when there was even half a choice.

Another tavern had tried to crop up a few years back that boasted better ale and finer women. But before it could take hold, a mysterious fire in the middle of the night had wiped it and its wares out in one blaze. The owner and 'fine women' split town and didn't bother to return. It was always suspected that it was set on purpose. But as anyone knew sometimes, bad shit just happened. No one had claimed to have any involvement, but then, if they had, they faced criminal action. No matter what the real story was, people kept their mouth shut in regards to whatever they did or didn't know. No other establishment had tried to set up since. It didn't seem wise under the circumstances.

So, she found herself lounging, brim of her cap shading her eyes, heavy boots propped up on the opposite chair crossed at the ankles, and watching the drunks begin to filter in, weary from the day. Some making passes at the soggy barmaid. Some regaling each other with slurred conversation. Occasionally, the door opened and more men would march in, and she'd stare in their direction looking for Brock. But he hadn't shown up yet.

She wasn't worried yet because it was likely he had been waiting far longer for her than she was for him. Everything took its time. It didn't mean that she liked it, but she had a secret to hide and she did the best she could to stay minimally exposed. She had grown used to the idea of waiting. Ed shifted on the hard chair beneath her, re-crossing her legs, hands folded in her lap. When she began to drift off to sleep, she felt the chair beneath her feet get kicked.

"This ain't no place to sleep."

Shaking her head to chase the fog of sleep away, Ed looked blearily up at the angry face of a blonde, haggard barmaid. Ed couldn't help but notice that she probably wanted to take a nap herself judging from the deep pockets under her eyes. Clearing her throat, Ed smiled sheepishly. "Just resting my eyes. Waiting on someone."

The barmaid's face didn't soften. "I don't care if you were waiting on the King, you can't sleep here. Are you done with that ale yet? Can't be hogging up this table for other paying customers."

Ed looked around. There were at least a dozen lopsided open tables and no real demand for the spaces. Lifting the heavy mug, she shook it. A resounding sloshing sound could easily be heard. "No. Still some left"

"If I see you sleeping again, you're getting the boot out of here...with or without your ale. We're not a church." She spun on her heel, but before she could leave, Ed put a hand out to catch her elbow. "Seen my business partner around here the last few days?

The woman looked as if she wouldn't answer. "Ach, come on now, I didn't mean anything by being tired. I've been sitting here waiting on my friend who hasn't shown up. I'm tired and angry on waiting for him to show. If you've seen him, maybe I can get out of here and find him if you know where he might be."

The woman pulled her arm out of Ed's grasp sneering down at the grimy sleeve of Ed's coat. Everyone had some kind of standards. "Stocky fellow? Brown hair, brown eyes, limps?"

Ed leaned across the table top, "Yeah, that's him. Big, brown moldy old coat?"

She pursed her lips. "Think I saw him three days ago. Came in here, took a table, and was here for a bit drinking. One of Lord Lockette's men came in asking for some volunteers for some job out on the estate. Your man, he spoke with Lord Lockette's skinny fellow and I ain't seen neither of them since."

Ed sat back feeling the hard wood against her shoulder blades. "This skinny Lord's man—he say what the job was? Or if he was coming back? He have a name?" Three days ago. So Brock had waited at least a day for her, if the old woman from the shack had counted the days right.

The barmaid shrugged her ample shoulders, "he didn't rightly say. Some men went with him and some stayed put. The Lord's man said his name was 'Mr. Swicker', he said he'd come back today and have a gander if anyone else was interested. Think he's been moving around looking for more men. Didn't get that many from here from what I could tell."

"I thank you for the mighty fine information. Think I'll wait a bit and see if this Mr. Swicker comes back. Then I'll be out of your hair." The barmaid walked away without any further acknowledgment and reported in to the bartender. They both looked at her while they talked quietly.

Licking her lips, she folded her hand around a mug of ale, lifted it, and drank. Ballocks, the ale was fusty. Absolutely rotten. Keeping her eye contact with the owner, she kept a straight face until he looked away. Then, she cringed and wiped her mouth on the inside collar of the coat. The sad thing was that it wasn't even the cheapest brew in the place. It was close, but the coin in her pocket and the rotten days she'd had, made her offer up a bit more money than the lowest stocked ale. It managed to get a person drunk well enough but the first mugs of it were the worst until the taste didn't matter anymore.

Adjusting her position, it took all of her strength to avoid falling asleep. Each time she felt the urge, she'd pinch herself hard to shake it off. It was quite a while before the wooden door creaked open again. By this time—with fresh bruises on her skin—the rain had stopped dripping through the roof; she hadn't noticed when it'd stopped.

The man who strode inside the tavern was a tall, thin, clean man dressed in much better clothing than anyone else in the shoddy place could afford to pay for. If he lingered past dark he'd be likely to be robbed. It was actually a small surprise that the man had even been able to walk inside the tavern at all without being accosted.

Men looked in his direction, dismissed him, and went back at their business of drinking as if knowing what he'd come for. And perhaps they did since they largely ignored him even as he scanned them all one by one.

"I am Mr. Albert Swicker. My Lord and Lady Lockette have sent me to request a few able bodies to do a bit of work. Are there any here who might be interested in such a request?"

As he made his announcement Ed noticed that the man managed to only elicit a few halfhearted shrugs in his direction. Most of the men had families to feed and farms to take care of in this part of the area, and not many were willing to give up a means of food unless a reward was well worth it. Food stock often was more valuable than coin could immediately provide. One couldn't eat money to survive.

In most cases, it wasn't worth it for them. But if they had grown sons, they might send them out to earn some extra money while an offer was available. This crowd didn't seem altogether eager by the frowns on their faces.

One man shouted out, "You was in here the other day. The men who wanted to go, went. They ain't back yet, so you have all that can be spared already. Leave us poor men to our drinkin'."

Ed saw the man named Swicker frown at the toothless fellow's outcry. Even for Ed, it'd been hard to understand what he'd said at first. Drunk and toothless was a misunderstanding waiting to happen. Catching his eye, Ed motioned to him. He quickly cut a path through the huddled figures and made straight for her table. Without speaking, she lifted her boots from the chair and pushed her mug at him to share her ale in hospitality. He sat down and leaned forward for the mug. If he were a high-born man, he wouldn't have bothered to touch the mug. But he inclined his head and lifted it. Seeing him closer up, she noticed some stubble on his chin and bags under his eyes. It seemed to be a common affliction.

Blanching after a swallow, he pushed it away like it was on fire. "Horse piss tastes better than that drivel."

Probably not altogether an untrue statement, but it was hard to tell, not having drunk any horse piss herself. Inclining her head to him she asked, "What is the job?"

He looked her over and made all the assumptions that she wanted him to make. Teenage boy. Dirty, swollen face, over-sized coat and boots. Probably his father's clothes. Poor. "Some animal attacks on the land. Lord Lockette wishes to slay them. A few staff members appear to have gone missing as well. Possibly related to the attacks. An investigation and hunt are being organized."

"Doesn't he already have men to do that?" She couldn't help but wonder why there was a need to hire outside men to do what the locals could do. As far as she knew, the estate was secluded and miles off in the country. Lock's Landing was named for Lord Lockette in hopes that he'd bring profit to the area, but he had never visited. Little wonder. He'd probably have run screaming in the other direction. Or worse, burn the entire place down.

He shrugged, not answering the question. It's the information that he'd been given. Who was he to question his Lord's written request? He picked at something on his handsome gentleman's coat and scanned the room to see if anyone else had shown interest in his announcement. "What's your interest? You look too young."

Ed shrugged. "I'm looking for a friend. Tallish, stocky man. Brown hair, brown eyes. Name's Thaddeus Brock. Goes by 'Brock' though. Heard you might have talked to him."

Swicker sat back and tried to remember the man in question. "I talked to a few men of that general description, yes. I did not get any names, though." If he had, he doubted he would have remembered them. He'd been all over the countryside looking for volunteers.

"Those men take on your job offer?"

"Several did, yes. I sent a group ahead of me, up to the estate."

Ed was not sure where to go from here. Brock had waited, but had moved on to a legitimate, available job. Did he still have her share left? It was difficult to know for sure. What she could relatively be sure of was that they wouldn't be body snatching before the sawbones came back into town. No place safe to keep the bodies. So that meant she could go after him, either to help him make more money for them to split or decide to move on by herself and forget about the coin altogether. Maybe cut her losses and leave the town of Lock's Landing behind her and travel onto Sindalberg to see if there was to be any money to be made there instead. It couldn't have been much coin for the one body...

"What kind of animal is it?"

"The kind that bites." Albert was tired and wanted to move on. Since Lock's Landing was the last stop he had to make before returning home, he just wanted to get it over with. He'd made no new prospects on this 'round and had almost skipped over a return stop. A few days of riding in the carriage or staying at local inns had left him with a powerful need to be home. And there was no way he was planning on staying in the The Slaughtered Goat's accommodations, whatever those might be—likely not very good based on the condition of the place. He glanced back at the swollen, dirty boy's face and sighed. It looked like he'd been on the receiving end of one heck of a fight. "We don't know what the animal is. That's part of the point. To hunt whatever it is down."

"If you need the extra hands, I'm free up."

Albert choked down the mirth in his throat. "I'm not sure this is work for a lad like you. Have you even fired a gun before?"

Ed feigned shock. "Be serious, sir. What kind of father wouldn't teach a son to shoot?" She honestly had never really learned. Guns were an expense that she could rarely afford. But it couldn't be hard. The dangerous end pointed outwards and she had to be careful not to shoot her own foolish foot off. She could learn.

"Where's your father now?"

Ed had the wherewithal to look saddened, casting a look skyward. "My family is dead. I have no one else and Brock is a friend. He'll put in a good word for me once we meet back up."

He peered closely at the boy weighing his words, "and how is it he left without your company?"

"We got separated and were supposed to meet up here. I believe he took you up on your opportunity before I could arrive. And he owes me some money that I could sure use."

She hoped.

Albert gave his full weight to the back of the chair contemplating the arrangement. The boy could be put to work with other tasks as well. He fingered a small flat button on the breast of his coat thinking of the list of work the boy could do. It was unlikely the hunting group would allow the boy along but if he could shoot well, they might reconsider it.

"Alright then. I have a carriage arriving shortly. I still have some business to conduct here." He reached for his coin purse, pushed back his chair, and stood.

Ed nodded, collected the coat around her, and rose to her feet as well, eyeing the coin purse with envy. "I could use some fresh air, Mr. Swicker."

"Excellent. I'll meet you out front, then. Shouldn't be long." Albert looked around and figured it wouldn't be long at all. These men had no real intentions of leaving their seats, let alone their homesteads in their present state. He hoped to grab a good stock of bread and decent ale at least before climbing back into the damnable confines of the carriage again. It didn't occur to him to share.

Ed stepped out into the air, scratching her nose and moving away from the tavern door. Her body ached. She'd been sitting for so long that she noticed with amusement that her back cheeks had gone numb. Rotating her shoulders to work the kinks out, she looked up at the dark sky.

She really had been waiting all day, it hadn't just felt like it. She rubbed a tired finger over the sleeve of the arm that she'd marked up trying not to sleep. Her body was a field of wounds from the past few days. She rubbed both hands over her face.

The hearty smell of stink, sewage, and sour food rose in her nostrils. The scent was familiar and not one particularly unwelcome. It was what she knew and she liked what felt like home. It was what she'd come accustomed to with all its quirks and ups and downs. Just not really the home of her dreams. Maybe some day she'd figure out where her dreams were leading her. Breathing deeply, she pulled in the night scents in around her.

Then she caught movement to her left.

Two skinny boys in tattered clothes emerged from beneath the low eave of a closed tailor shop not far from where she stood. Their faces were gaunt and smudged with dirt as they watched her with a haunted expression. She looked the kids over and then discreetly checked the other shadows where people might be hiding as she pretended to pat her pockets.

The boys meant trouble. Though she didn't know if they were here for her. They were particularly dangerous to rich drunkards and maybe they'd mistaken her for Swicker. There were a few kids' gangs that roamed the streets looking for easy marks. The majority of them comprised of orphans, who took on big fish for a bigger profit; higher profile people like Swicker seemed to be, but some were not so choosy. As was obvious in the choice of their current target.

Most of the gangs ranged with children easily between six and eleven years old, and they learned from each other. It was hunger and desperation that made the kids a dangerous bunch, using anything sharp or crude as tools to take whatever they wanted from their victims. If they could eat it, sell it, wear it, or make something from it, they considered it all in a day's work. No remorse. If they were lucky enough to kill a victim, they'd haul the body in for the coin—dragging the sorry corpse shamelessly along the street—each child with a handful of whatever the poor sod was left wearing.

Ed nodded at the boys, hoping this exchange wasn't going to result in a fight. The elder of the two boys pushed a lad forward no older than six, his face smudged with so much dirt it'd looked as if he'd been eating a pile, nose first.

"Have some coins...to spare for our hungry stomachs?"

Carefully, she regarded the young face and turned out her empty coat pockets in a slow deliberate move. She'd managed to spend what she had on the ale. "Nothing."

The elder boy grunted and pushed forward in a jerky move elbowing the little one aside. "Bollocks you have nothing. You've been in there all bloody day. That's as good as yelling to the rooftops that you've got deep hidden pockets as sure as anything I've seen." His speech was broken as he talked

Whoops. "You're wrong. Shove off."

"That's as grand as a pretty gold coin! I'm the one wrong? Your arse barely left the table the entire day. We seen you."

"I drank one cup the entire day. Tavern isn't happy about it neither. You can ask them."

A look of uncertainty graced the face of the youngest but the eldest was determined. "You gotta give us something. We'ze starving."

"There's nothing to give."

A rock flew out of nowhere grazing Ed's ear, narrowly missing her swollen cheek. She swore and jerked a hand up to hold her wounded ear. She glared into the darkness where it'd come from. A second one, smaller than the first, was launched from the right, striking her above the knee and bounced off into the dirt. Clenching her teeth, she watched a scattered band of boys emerge from both directions. "We be Jack's gang." One boy boasted proudly.

"I have no trinkets, coins, or shiny stuff. Clothes is it." She pulled at the fabric of her pants trying to reason with the boys again and sighed. "Let me see Jack and I'll have a go at him." Nothing about the last few days had been easy. Her body hurt enough already with all of the wounds she'd collected. She didn't understand why she couldn't get a break. This was a perfect example of why she needed Brock's bulk to ward off trouble. She was too small and skinny and looked the perfect victim to mess with.

A few of the boys laughed in unison at her response. She knew that the safest thing to do would be to go back inside and await her escort rather than fight these boys. One or two, maybe. But not a gang. As she turned to go back inside, she noticed two dirty boys with thick clumps in their hair had snuck up behind her. Bold as anything the shortest boys fist punched her in the crotch.

The pain was jarring. Regardless that she did not have the necessary parts, the unexpected jolt to such a sensitive area was truly stunning. She had a fleeting thought of so this is what it's like. It was as if a musket had gone off in her pants. The sucker punch to her jaw came from the other kid and, as she fell backwards, a hand went for the dagger. All that she had, all that she owned, she wore. She wasn't about to let these small thieves take what she had easily. Last time was bad enough and the little shits would quickly find out her gender if they stripped her clothes as well.

Several boys jumped at her immediately as she fell. Her cap fell off as she landed. She could feel rough little hands patting her down looking for pockets. Bloody blooming flaming Hell. Throwing an arm over her face, she felt new kicks to her ribs along with a few boys who piled onto her legs to try to immobilize her. Flailing and rolling, she pinned a few of them to the ground, using her knife to make her point known. More kids leapt onto her back trying to hold her down. As she made hers, they also made theirs with sharp objects of their own. Was that a needle weapon? Ed winced feeling the thin edge slide in and out of her legs as she struggled against them.

Ed stabbed one boy through the hand and he gritted his teeth at her as he slapped the blade from her fist and then slugged her in the stomach with his uninjured hand. Another boy had some kind of heavy object and was banging at her shin with it. His thin, tan face grinning wickedly showing off his missing bottom teeth as he continued making a solid bruise on her. When she felt the tugging on the coat, she swore and struggled to stop them from taking it. Not the coat!

Arms and legs were everywhere as a flurry of punches and kicks came from all directions. Surrounded and overwhelmed, she grunted and swore loudly, pushing against her small assailants from the ground. Her movements were not helpful to her cause as the boys managed to peel the coat down and off her arms as she flailed. She felt the cool air replace the lining of the coat and she made an angry noise. They ran away with it, snickering as they went. "Little stinking bastards!" She'd really liked that coat.

A new boy, with skin so dark that he didn't look real, parted a sea of flying elbows and legs and came to sit on her chest, his bony butt cheeks digging into her. She stopped struggling, gasping for breath as he grinned maniacally into her face. A gleaming straight edged blade in his small hands. "I'm Jack Baker. These are my boys. I like your coat." He spoke with an accent that she didn't recognize and leaned forward, bracing his elbows on his knees pressing his buttocks deeper into her chest making it hard to breathe. Jack stared down into her face, rubbing the edge of the blade in front of her eyes with his the pad of his thumb. Beads of blood welled up and he showed it to her, leaned forward and smeared it on her forehead. Ed swallowed staring up at Jacks knife.

Then suddenly, bodies began disappearing. She tensed, raising her arms bracing for a fight and almost slugged her savior. He stood above her frowning down as he shucked each wiggling boy from her, throwing them wide like sacks of wheat. She balled her fist and punched the last boy that lay on her, but he wasn't Jack. Jack had darted off into the shadows. Protected and watching. For the last lad, the man gave an extra shove with his boot. "Bunch of hooligans. What is this area coming to?"

Leaning down, Swicker extended a hand and grabbed Ed under the elbow and pulled her up as if she weighed nothing. The fresh blood and bruises protested as she leaned over and snatched up her cap that had ended up beneath her.

Grimacing, she inclined her aching head, acknowledging his assistance. The new blows to her head were not helping the ones she'd already had. Small white spots were forming before her eyes and she grabbed a hold of her inner elbow through her shirt and pinched hard to avoid flatly passing out and humiliating herself further. She was going to get a reputation of an easy mark if this kept up. Well, easier, any way.

"You seem to attract trouble, my young friend."

He didn't know the half of it. "Bloody kids."

"I should say. That band of misfits should all be hanged." Albert looked around and saw the kids staring from the darkness and they snarled back at him like a pack of wild dogs. "Be off with you!" He flicked his hand in their direction as if they were servants that would listen, but the children stayed and continued to watch them with eerie quiet, teeth bared.

One boy held up the stolen coat by the collar with a finger and redness stained her cheeks as she intended to advance on him. Swicker grabbed her arm by the elbow before she could take two steps. Perhaps it was fortunate that the sound of horses approached when they did because Ed wanted to get her coat back. The tightening of Swicker's hand did little to squelch her inner most thirst to get it from the kid. Blast it all. From the darkness of the lane, a black carriage sporting lanterns emerged in front of the tavern.

Swicker withdrew a handkerchief from a pocket and passed it to Ed. "Normally, I'd ask a personage like yourself to ride up front with the driver. But seeing as though you've been attacked in the dirt, I'm feeling a bit soft knowing you were mauled and robbed on my watch. Seeing as though I am yet again empty handed anyway. I'll allow you ride inside the carriage with me."

Ed made a rude noise, took the extended cloth, and wiped her forehead with it. "I don't need no special seats, Mr. Swicker." She handed it back to him and he frowned down at it and let it fall to the ground. She started to walk toward the front of the carriage when Swicker picked her up bodily and all but tossed her inside the carriage.

"Stupid stubborn child."

"I—"

Swicker waved a hand in her direction to silence her, climbed inside, and closed the door behind him. "That's settled." Dropping onto the opposite seat, he stared out of the window. "If I never see this place again, it will be too soon," he muttered, resting his back against the rich red color of the seat and closing his eyes. "The seats aren't overly comfortable, but the ride is a bit of a stretch...so feel free to catch some sleep. Don't bother pick-pocketing me. I am armed and I won't hesitate to use it if I feel the slightest of movement of my clothes, is that understood?" He cracked open an eye to look in her direction.

Ed shifted on the seat hiding a wince at the new injuries. Swicker was right. The seat was hardly better than the inn chair she'd sat in all day. The biggest difference was the red soft covering. It didn't do much for comfort though. Her buttocks still protested as she tried to find a spot left that didn't make all of her injuries ache. A few moments later, it turned out just as well that she was inside as it started to rain again. If nothing else, she'd be dry for the trip.

She looked at Swicker and shrugged. What did he expect her to say, that she planned on robbing him blind and leaping like a lunatic from the moving carriage? "Sure."

He nodded, rested his head back, and seemingly fell asleep. Exhausted, but not yet willing to let herself trust a man she just met, she stared out the window without seeing anything as her mind began to go over the events of the past few days. She wished that she hadn't lost the goddamn coat. The knife was gone too, but the coat had been extra nice. She shifted on the seat, folding her arms over her stomach, and listened to the raindrops fall against the roof.

7

Esther carried her shoes close to her bosom with a bag of food over her shoulder as she ran down the hallway. The food bumped and shifted against her back as she moved.

The night that Richard had killed Molly had been the longest one of her life as she waited out the screams and moaning sounds starting to come from the courtyard. Her stomach had begun to make hungry noises long before the screaming had stopped. After a while, everything had gone eerily silent and she waited there formulating a plan.

She was awake when rays came through the window announcing that dawn had arrived. By that time she'd ruled out trying to climb from the window unless it was a last resort. She may be rich by association, ergo on the naive side, but she wasn't a stupid woman. She knew her limitations and needed to compensate for them. Any scenario that she envisioned, the idea of climbing out of it ended up with her in various stages of falling from the rain-soaked eaves, either to an immediate death or falling and her broken body being discovered by Richard and eaten alive in the mud. She wouldn't have believed it if she hadn't seen it with her own horrified eyes, but that's what he'd done: eaten someone alive. Esther shuddered, remembering the expression she'd seen gleaming from him. He'd enjoyed it, which sickened her even further. She had started to imagine Richard's deranged face on each monster that would come at her.

In her mind, she knew that Richard was safely locked away in their bedroom, but there was no mistaking the sounds she'd heard through the night. There were more like him out there. More sick people. It made her feel miserable that she'd laughed about his illness to his face. Whether it was being bitten or an infection from something else, he was truly sick and she had mocked her own husband.

Esther knew that she had to do something instead of sit and wait it out until someone showed up with food so she began looking for some kind of weapon. There were no traditional ones to speak of since Richard made sure that guns and swords were locked away in the armory on the lower level of the estate. Her gaze shifted to ornaments, bottles of various shapes, to bowls and a water pitcher. There were plenty of bobbles that she might be able to throw at an attacker, but she rather doubted that it would slow them down for long. Not with the determined madness she'd seen in Richard's eyes.

If only the room had a fireplace, she might have been able to take a poker from it to wield, though the idea of her striking out with one seemed more a comedy than reality. She had no real strength to fend someone off. Muscles on a Lady was considered unattractive and unnecessary. It didn't matter, seeing as this room had been deemed far too small for a fireplace anyway.

Scanning the room, her gaze fell upon the matching candleholder set. She didn't know where they'd come from, probably a previous wife judging by the rose pattern engraved into the sides, but they were made of heavy silver. They were thick at the base and skinny at the top, and if pressed to, she might be able to use one as a makeshift club. It would have to do under the circumstances since there was little else to rely on. She was confident that could always upgrade if she found something better to use instead.

A petite bloodstained figure standing in the middle of a child's guest room, she knew with striking clarity that she didn't qualify as someone who could defend herself very well, but she'd simply have to try. Esther's sense of dignity reminded her that she just couldn't be seen running around in her unmentionables doing it either. Heat raced across her cheeks burning a path down her neck knowing that she needed to rectify her clothing situation. Her gaze traveled along the room looking for something to use. Quickly, she crossed to the bed throwing back the blanket. She pulled at the bedding feeling the muscles in her arms strain to extract a sheet from the mattress. Then she grasped a bed sash. Wrapping the sheet around her form, she tucked the edges into her corset and secured it at the waist with the sash. It wouldn't do for the High Ladies of court, but in a pinch, it would have to do.

Satisfied that she was modestly covered, Esther stepped over to the large ornate dresser and removed the candle from a holder, setting it down where it promptly rolled off and onto the floor. Shaking her head with annoyance, she picked the holder up by the thin end and began making experimental test swings.

Yes. She'd do it if she had to.

She'd have to be practical, of course. She certainly didn't want to die, so she'd do what she had to in order to survive. If she could run instead like she had before, she'd take that option, instead. Given the success of her escaping her mad husband before, running certainly seemed less difficult than if she'd stood there and beaten him with a candle stick holder.

She moved to the door and pressed her ear to the wood to listen if anything lay beyond it. Hearing nothing, she unlocked it then pulled it open and peered out, candleholder ready to be swung. The hallway seemed empty. All the doors still appeared closed.

Relaxing her arm, she opened the door wider, satisfied that she wasn't stepping into a crowd of sickly madmen. She rotated her shoulder to relax it from the weight of her weapon born of circumstance and then reached out to pull the door closed behind her. She didn't want any nasty surprises inside waiting for her when she got back to the room.

Esther walked forward on the tips of her boots like a cat walking on soft paws. The hallway looked much the same as it always had, but she knew behind some of these doors, things were less than the normal. Eyeing a particular door, she crept past where Richard was captive. She was startled to feel a sense of pride in herself, knowing that she'd managed to keep him behind a closed door even in a panic like that. At the time, she thought he'd just pull open the door and continue coming at her, but he hadn't. It seemed as if he'd forgotten how to use the door, which was more than fine by her. She doubted she could have outrun him beyond the hallway.

She noticed that as the shouting had gone on earlier, she'd been able to hear Richard banging against his door trying to get out. As if he wanted to participate in the human hunt going on around him. He'd always been a big hunting fan. But now with things quiet around the estate she hadn't heard him for hours.

Was he dead? Sleeping it off? She hesitated for a moment, but couldn't take a chance on checking to see how he was and moved on. She'd need protection before she would have the courage to look him in the eyes again. She couldn't risk that he might be sitting on the bed staring at the door waiting for it to be opened. Shivering at the thought, she knew it was better to wait for some strong men who could overpower him if he was still not himself.

If it was a sickness, perhaps there was a cure that would return him to health. The whole incident would have to be covered up of course. He'd attacked and killed at least Molly, if not the unfortunate soul in the kitchens. The estate would be lucky to get staff after an event like this if word got out.

A lot of money would have to exchange hands, but it could be 'swept under the rug', as they say. The Lockette estate was well out of the view of the courts and they might slide by without notice. If the past night's transgression was found out, she wasn't sure what would happen to her then.

For now, she just had to wait until the men she'd called on for aid arrived. Which she hoped was soon. She was a Lady and was certainly not used to any of this mayhem. It was beneath her and she wanted someone else to come along so that she could tell them what to do for her.

This time when Esther reached the stairs, there were no sounds coming from below. Hesitating for a moment, she glanced back at the room at the end of the hall that she'd found safety in. If she only could just hide there until help arrived. Her lips tightened at the thought. It was the safest idea and the urge was strong to go back and hide. But then, so was the urge to eat.

Esther braced her back against the wall of the staircase and descended step by step. The beautiful and elaborate paintings that hung on the staircase were thankfully hung higher than her head so she wasn't hitting any of them as she went along. Richard had spent a small fortune on them and wouldn't take kindly to them being damaged. Not by anyone.

She was gripping the candleholder against her chest, listening for any sound when her knees threatened to buckle beneath her. Pushing herself ramrod straight against the wall, she reminded herself that she was the Lady of the house and her fear, while warranted, could not get in the way of her objective. She wasn't sure what she'd find when she reached the main hallway but whatever it was, she'd handle it. There was no other way.

Esther took her time, but finally reached the bottom of the staircase. Light from the windows around the door poured in casting a warm hue around the room. Fine tapestries and elegant portraits lined the walls in a pleasant arrangement. It was a beautiful room in which she often marveled when she saw it. It held a welcome there that wasn't matched from the staff but when she'd first arrived, it had felt like home. Too bad the overall feeling had been short lived.

Esther peered around the polished stone floor noting that several miniature statues had been knocked from their perches and had broken into many pieces on the floor. For a moment, she felt a burst of anger in her chest seeing them scattered like that all over the entryway and she opened her mouth to call for a maid. Then, she remembered the situation and closed her mouth noting that the ones that hadn't been merely knocked off their stands, in broken heaps, might have been thrown instead. To ward off an attacker? Esther thought of the way Richard had leapt out from the darkness and maybe if she'd been holding something, maybe she would have thrown it too.

Feeling her temper dissipate she stepped off the last stair. There were four doorways off the main entryway. Easily recognizable as the 'heart' of the house. The opening that she wanted was on the left side, but a trail of blood on the floor drew her gaze towards the study on the right, where a body in a dress was laying face down just beyond the open doorway. The shoes were highly worn and the skirt was bunched around a pair of stocking clad knees, having fluttered there when she'd fallen.

Appalled, Esther stepped back against the wall to add some distance between them. It was hard to tell with her face down, but she was had an impression the girl had been one of the younger maids being trained for higher services within the household. Esther squinted and tried to remember what her name might have been out of morbid curiosity. Lacy...Lissa...or maybe Lily? No, it wasn't any of those. Something starting with an "L" though. As she stared at the body, it didn't occur to her to go over to see if the girl was all right but it was hard not to stare, all the same.

With nothing that she could do since the girl was obviously beyond her help, Esther opened the door to the kitchen and marched through, then blinked at the destruction that greeted her. *There'd been quite a fight in here*, she thought, moving forward and staring at the widespread mess. Bags of cooking supplies were open and spilling onto the ground with large gashes in their portly sides. Pots looked as if they'd been weapons or metal missiles as they littered the area. Fruit, vegetables, and even chunks of raw meat were strewn around and squished against the floor as if a stew had exploded and a herd of cattle had run through the area flattening everything. Not cattle. Shoes. Human shoes. The staff had been running for their lives.

If it weren't for the smudged bloody handprints, red dragging smear marks, and splatters of blood covering the surfaces, she could have thought a gigantic food fight had taken place instead. Shaking her head at the colossal waste of resources, Esther rushed forward to begin collecting up undamaged food. Fruits and raw vegetables came first. The meats she'd have to leave behind because there was no way to cook them, even if she wanted to.

When it became clear that her arms couldn't hold enough items, she crossed and tipped over a bag of unopened grain onto the floor, emptying it amidst the other unusable food. Stepping around the new mess, she deposited her armload and then she ducked and weaved around the room, gathering everything she could and piling it into the bag gently.

Esther was bent over to grab a loaf of bread when she heard a noise behind her. Bread loaf forgotten, she turned to see where it had come from and she was surprised to see the fallen "L" girl leaning against the doorway.

Like Molly, the girl's throat had been torn out. Large, pink, fleshy, loose flaps of skin had been peeled away exposing a red and black looking mess. Chunks of her neck were completely missing and the damage trailed down the front of her gown, along with much of her face. Dried blood smeared her skin like war paint in places where it still showed and her loose hair was matted in a tangled mess of frizz as if her head had been rubbed repeatedly against a wool rug. One eyeball was missing, looking as if it might have been popped somewhere along the attack. A thick white eggy looking mess combined with blood hung down around her cheek.

The girl's nose was gone, leaving a gaping black hole in the center of her face, as well as most of the flesh from her lips. The girl raised a badly bitten bare arm. The circular bite wounds had called blood to the surface of her skin, each one punctuating the horror of her attack. She'd been held down and bitten into, some abrasions obviously more successful in damaging her than others. She dropped her arm, moaned and staggered forward wobbling on unsteady legs.

Esther's mind reeled in that moment.

If she turned away from this girl who needed help, which she desperately wanted to do, would God forgive her for such an act? Helping was the last thing that she wanted to do but her mind could not fathom how else the girl could be walking if she were not alive and in need of help. She took a tentative step forward and then stopped. Esther stooped to retrieve the food bag from the floor in a classic this is mine gesture and placed it closer, to further lay claim to the contents. She wasn't about to share with a servant. There was plenty of other food spread around the room that was likely that the girl knew how to cook, unlike Esther herself.

As the girl got closer the sight of her made Esther want to take her bag and run away but she steeled herself. The girl was a victim, not an ill madman the way her husband had been. No matter how Esther had been treated, a Lady didn't shirk her responsibilities. Food bag aside, it was her duty to Richard to be strong in his absence. Esther frowned as she saw someone else move into the doorway just beyond the girl's shoulder.

Garrity was an elderly footman and had been with them shortly after her marriage to Richard, after the previous footman had passed away. Richard had located him while he attended a meeting with another prominent family and had outright purchased the man's services rather than promote a new footman within his own household. Something about the man had grabbed Richard's attention. Garrity was perhaps the only one in Richard's employ that wasn't brutally indifferent to her. Oh, he wasn't overly nice to her either, as that might imply something wholly inappropriate, but occasionally he would smile in her direction and say a kind word here and there—like a distant grandfather might.

It was clear that he'd been attacked as well. His face was bloody and gnawed upon, tufts of grey hair bunched at the top of his head and as he shuffled closer, it looked as if some of his teeth had been knocked out. His clothes were dirty and torn, coat hanging in tatters from his shoulders. He reached a hand out toward her from his position and she was revolted to see that several fingers on his hand were missing, congealed bloody stumps waving at her like fat sausages as he grabbed air. Then, he growled at her like a mutt.

Esther stepped carefully backwards, puzzled at his behavior. When he broke into a sprint, he knocked the struggling "L" girl aside and lurched at Esther. Dismayed, Esther slapped his outstretched hands away before he managed to grab her and she looked around frantically for the candleholder. She'd put it down next to her when it got in the way of picking up the scattered food. Grabbing at it from the counter, she gulped and swung it striking only air at first. "Stay back! I'll club you with this if I have to." She managed to keep her internal panic out of her tone.

He grabbed at her again, his stubby fingers brushing her arm. Esther sucked her bottom lip into her mouth, and she swung as hard as she was able to at his outstretched hand, knocking it away. He growled at her, reaching with the other arm. "I mean it! Stop this at once!"

The thick base of the candleholder caught him on the side of the head this time and he staggered back and fell onto his backside, subsequently making the girl who'd gotten closer behind him, trip. The girl fell over Garrity's legs and she lashed out, catching the hem of Esther's makeshift dress and began pulling on the material. Esther kicked at the girl but Esther didn't have much force in the kick and the scamp wouldn't let go of the hem. As Esther struggled to stay on her feet, she swung the candleholder with more controlled motions trying to make a connection.

Garrity began to rise from his position, tossing the girl off him; but he also managed to push her a little bit closer to Esther. Shouting in panic, Esther struck low, managing to hit Garrity as the candleholder passed him. She lost her grip and it flew heavily across the room and bounced off the large cooking pot making a loud noise. Esther gapped at her misfortune, her gaze immediately going to the two staff members. Momentarily distracted by the noise, the two wounded staff members stared at where the sound had come from.

Taking the opportunity, Esther grabbed at the sack of food and began backpedaling away from the both of them. She dragged the distracted girl, who was still holding onto her sheet dress, across the floor with her. Twirling, Esther saw that Garrity had begun to dismiss the noise of the candleholder and was stumbling closer. She tore at the sash of the dress with her fingers, working quickly to untie it. It came off easily and the girl fell back with an armful of the sheet.

Esther jumped backwards scanning for the door to the stables, leaped toward it, and pulled the door open with her free hand. Trembling, she turned and re-enacted her escape with Richard by slamming the door closed before Garrity could get to her. Spinning, she looked around her and almost screamed when she saw four stable boys surrounding a dead horse. They were pulling at the animal's innards and shoving handfuls into their mouths. She swallowed back the sound and was glad that she hadn't given into hysteria. Esther stepped quickly away from the door while the boys were distracted. A raunchy smell was in the air and she had a sinking feeling that she now knew what the combination of horse feces and blood smelled like.

Feeling dizzy, Esther skirted past them as she heard the door being struck behind her. She picked up speed and began to run openly through the stables feeling fatigued even with the minimal effort. She sailed past a mostly naked maid who for all appearances had been in the process of a sexual encounter when she'd been killed. Esther's boots struck loud against the stable floor as she ran through blood and straw.

Reaching the courtyard of the estate she noted deep gouges in the ground, straw littered in frenzied directions, and random strips of cloth strewn around. She had no time to dwell on the unkempt mess and though the disorder nipped at her mind she was more interested in getting back to safety. She winced at the feeling in her feet. They were stinging because her boots had not been made for running of any kind and the pinching along the sides were beginning to cause blisters. With the sounds of being chased echoing behind her, Esther pushed aside the discomfort and dashed toward the manor. She skidded to stop at the stairs that led up to the main entryway. Quickly, she unlaced her boots and slipped them off so that she could run faster and, she hoped, be quieter on the stone when she got back inside. Food bag slung over her shoulder, her boots crushed against her chest, she pushed the door open. Nothing greeted her, to which she felt some degree of relief. Esther glanced left and right before darting toward the steps leaving the door wide open.

The threat behind her, out in the courtyard now by the sounds of it, she moved as fast as she could. She took two steps to a time despite her fatigue, trying to break get beyond their eyesight so that maybe they wouldn't follow her to the bedroom door that she was hiding in. It was possible to choose another bedroom, but she couldn't be sure that all rooms were free of these...whatever they were. She knew the one she'd left had been clear of them and it was the one she wanted to get back to.

It hadn't been a clean trip, but she had chanced it anyway and for the most part had won a new victory to be proud of. Maybe she could take care of herself after all. So, she'd lost the candleholder and her makeshift dress...now she had food. It would have to be enough for now.

Rain had a way of making things more miserable. It dripped, splashed, and made everything dreary. Ed observed it all; from the carriage wheels splashing through the deep puddles, to the heavy sound striking the leaves around them. The first and likely the last, carriage ride that she had the lucky fortune to ride in and all the bloody wet stuff did was pound against the rooftop without stopping. Sometimes, drops angled inside the large window peppering her face when she managed to drift off, jerking her awake. What should have been the most privileged experience of her life was nothing more than all the crappy moments in her life; grueling and tiresome. She wondered why she should feel so disappointed with that. Expecting more out of her life often led to heartache anyway. She should be used to that idea by now.

The time passed slowly leaving Ed little else to do but keep replaying the events of the last days wishing things had gone differently. She hoped that she was making the right choice. If she had to walk back to town tomorrow because Brock decided his gig was well and good without her, it would take twice as long to regret and then take back her current choice. She could hardly expect a carriage ride to return her to town, which meant she'd be walking back with or without Brock and it'd still likely be bloody raining.

She could just imagine the look on Brock's face when she showed up, which is what kept her going. Well, the look on his face and her money. Her back up plan was to find out if she could stay on for some odd jobs and earn some pay before she moved on. She couldn't assume Brock had the money or that he'd be glad to see her. Of course, she didn't really blame him for having moved on, but he still owed her share of the haul. Whether he'd see it that way or not, only the future could tell.

A loud jarring snort from the other side of the carriage attracted her attention and she shifted her gaze in Swicker's direction and glowered. He was still asleep and had been since they'd left Lock's Landing. She envied that he had taken so many carriage rides in his life that he had figured out a way to actually get some sleep in one. To her, it seemed an impossible thing to do.

Bitter and exhausted Ed turned to face the window again, praying they'd get to their destination soon or that the rain would stop. She actually started to worry that she'd go mad and truly pitch herself from the moving torture device on wheels. Before, the idea had been amusing. Not so much anymore.

When they pulled up in front of the dark manor hours later it was still dark. The weather had not improved, therefore Ed had not slept. It wasn't lost on her that she'd slept for four days prior to the current damnable day she'd had today, but currently she felt like she hadn't slept in a week. Peering through miserably bleary, bloodshot eyes she took in the exterior of the imposing structure and made a face. Grasping the edge of the window she pulled herself forward scanning the darkness. Rain fell on her face as she stared. It didn't feel right. It certainly didn't look right.

There were no lamps lit, only the ones that the driver had lit for their passage. The courtyard looked as if someone had strewn hay all over the ground and the front door to the manor was wide open.; beyond that held nothing but pitch-darkness. For a reason that she couldn't explain, the image gave her chills. She'd have expected a Lord's estate to be much safer looking than this. Swicker had said there were animal attacks on the land. What kind of animals exactly, and had they gotten into the manor? Ed began to think coming here was a huge mistake, Brock or not, and she moved from the window and started to shift toward the exit. Maybe if she slunk away now it would be worth leaving anything Brock might have behind. Ed wasn't a hero. If animals were attacking people and they'd massacred the estate, she didn't want to be here when daylight hit the courtyard.

Swicker must have felt the shift in the carriage when she moved because his eyes shot open and he stared at her in confusion. He cleared his throat peering at her as if he was either surprised Ed was still there or couldn't remember who she was.

Instead of feeling embarrassed at having been caught sneaking away, she felt her annoyance at him creep back and crossed her arms over her flattened chest and produced a dirty look. She would have loved to punch the rested smile off his face. How dare he have the gall to look so totally rested after such a crap ride?

"Did you get any sleep?" Swicker asked, straightening in his seat and smoothing down his clothing.

"Does a Lady shit in the woods?" Ed snapped. If she didn't feel like there were mud patties in her eyes, she might have worded it differently, but it was too late to take it back.

Swicker blinked at her vulgarity and then seemed to consider her question. He barked a shout of laughter that echoed off the carriage walls and the sound mocked her. "You have spunk, kid. Better watch that around the estate, though. Not many people are used to spunk around here. To answer your question and acknowledge your answer, I suppose, that means 'no'." He had the decency to look apologetic. "I've had many years of practice sleeping in a carriage and have been away from the estate a few days traveling, so I suppose that has allowed me some tolerance of the means travel. I hadn't given it any thought that you wouldn't be used to it or I would have tried to stay awake."

Softening, Ed shrugged, "I'm a no one. Wouldn't have been a need." It didn't stop her from being jealous that he'd been able to get some shut-eye though. The flaming prick.

"Perhaps not, though it might have at least been a polite thing to have done." He leaned forward and peered out of the carriage. Almost immediately the door came open and the driver's form filled the space carrying a lantern. "Mr. Swicker, something doesn't seem right."

Swicker frowned and exited quickly. Wanting nothing more than to leave the carriage, Ed was only a step behind him and she nearly fell on him when he stopped directly in her path. Swicker's hand shot out and grabbed her shoulder before she could topple onto him.

Ed looked around the grounds and felt a cold feeling settle over her. She'd never been into religion one way or the other, belief never put food on her table, but she didn't like the sensation in the slightest. Something didn't seem right. The most disturbing part was why the door to a fancy estate would be wide open in the middle of the night for anyone to walk right in. With no one to guard it or come to see who'd arrived. Their carriage would have been viewable from at least half a mile off, and yet there was no one. It was no warm welcome, whatever Swicker had believed to be true upon their arrival. She'd never seen any place like this; both great and terrifying at the same time.

With a grim look on his face, he spoke to the driver. "Mr. Barlowe, seeing as though it is the very dead of night, please escort this young man to the servants' quarters off of the stables for the night." Ed opened her mouth to start to ask about Brock, but Swicker held up a finger and inclined his head toward her. "I understand your desire to find your companion, but I have no intention to wake everyone for a cheery late night reunion. Besides, you could use the sleep and probably something to eat before dawn breaks. And I need to..." he trailed off, "see about the manner to which I've returned to."

The rain cooled her heated skin as swayed on her feet. She was wary to let Swicker know how much she was dying to close her eyes and fall asleep. She could have gleefully curled up into a ball in the middle of the courtyard and slept with the rain making her shrivel like pruned fruit if Swicker hadn't been there. The swelling of her face when they first met didn't add to her case either. She did not want to show him anymore weakness. He'd already seen her rump get handed to her by a bunch of street kids and the thought didn't settle well in her stomach. It galled her to have needed help from the tangle of dirty street kids.

Catching herself in a stumble that she tried to pass off as moving away from Swicker, she forced herself to shrug as if she didn't care one way or the other. Whether the movement was noticed or not was hard to tell since her eyes felt as though they were ready to crawl out of her sockets and cheerfully soak up the rain.

"Now, Ed, please follow Mr. Barlowe and he will see you put up for the night." Swicker gave her a small push in the man's direction. Barlowe was tall, with a thick bulging waistline that implied he ate well regularly. He stared down at her with an annoyed look on his face. He had perhaps expected disheveled men from Lock's Landing, but not a skinny kid to journey with Swicker. He looked unsure as to why this boy had been brought along to begin with. Ed mirrored his expression as she looked back at him.

"This way," Barlowe said, a corner of his mouth upturned in a sneer. When they moved away from Swicker, who was watching them as they walked away, Barlowe whispered down at Ed, "I have my eye on you, kid. If anything goes missing around here, I'm coming after you."

Ed yawned, unimpressed with his threat, and so exhausted that the large boots on her feet caused her to misstep and lurch forward. "Other than people, you mean?" Barlowe grunted when Ed gestured around the courtyard. Glaring down at her, he pushed her small form ahead of him. *If only I was bigger...no one would push me around,* she thought bitterly.

Barlowe opened the stable door and motioned for Ed to go first. The room behind the stables was no prize, and it smelled of wet hay and horse manure, but it was still better than some places that Ed had been forced to find sleep in. That awful goat shack. At least the rain could not get through the roof of this place...and that was a big plus. Rain was most definitely on her naughty list. Barlowe motioned to the back of the stables as Ed trudged along, boots dragging, with a mix of pride and exhaustion marching her forward. Just a little farther...

She glanced at Barlowe who gestured impatiently at a door off to the side of the large stables and rolled his eyes as if she should have known where they were going. Sliding the door the door aside, she peeked in. A lamp was burning low and three cots with blankets were spread around the room. In the center of the room, bread and cheese had fallen on the floor while a mug remained upright on the table. Throwing a disgusted look at Barlowe, she stepped inside. Of course she would need to eat her meal off the ground. Why would she have expected to find it sitting upright on the table? Factoring in the cots, and counting the bread and cheese on the floor, it was obvious that they had been expecting more men to arrive with Swicker.

Barlowe grunted at her and, without another word, closed the door behind him. Quickly, she crossed to the table and squatted near the food collecting it all and placing it on the table. Finding a cheese knife near a table leg on the floor, she picked it up and looked it over. It wasn't very sharp but the blade was new and of fine quality as far as she could tell. Until she could get it sharpened better, the tip would do. Or she'd have to press real hard to cut anything. She glanced around and upon seeing no one, slipped it into her pocket.

Ed reached for the mug and found it half full. She barely tasted the bitter ale. Then Ed attacked the dirty cheese and bread using her fingers, with the mind set of a person who had been on the borderline of starvation. The bread was rough because it'd been left out in the air but her teeth tore through it not wanting to waste time to soften it. She swallowed and pushed a whole wedge of cheese in her mouth next and moaned at the sharp taste bursting in her mouth. Regardless of how she'd found it, it was far better food than she'd eaten in weeks and she began chewing faster, stuffing her mouth rapidly. No wonder Brock had volunteered his services. He must have known the estate had good digs.

Slurping the ale from the mug, she looked around the dim room and she wondered if Brock was right now, sleeping in a similar room somewhere on the grounds.

Not long after she ate, she realized that her bladder was begging for release. She looked for some place private. She wasn't accustomed to using chamber pots, given that the majority of places that she slept in were public, so she wasn't sure where she should look for one. She'd always found a quiet place away from prying eyes and used nature's toilet.

She wondered if Barlowe was guarding the door. The problem with finding a suitable place to urinate was the possibility of someone coming in through the door at the wrong moment. She had, years ago, perfected urinating standing up, but it still required some finesse and privacy. The idea was, in the extreme circumstances where she couldn't squat, to do so standing up. Over time she had started to do it all the time to help keep with the role of being male. The risk was still high that she could be seen, but not as high as if she squatted when she thought no one was around.

Walking to an empty corner nearest the door, her boots kicked something on the floor. The clatter startled her momentarily, but the tinny sound assured her that someone somewhere had known it was a good place to put a chamber pot. Luckily it hadn't seemed to have been used yet. Otherwise, in the best case scenario, right now she'd have had urine all over her boots.

As she watched the door like a hawk, she quickly untied the double-knot in her trousers, pushed the material aside, stuck two fingers inside to position herself to help guide the stream of urine. Then she pushed out hard with her stomach muscles. Exhaling with a sense of satisfaction at the pressure diminishing in her bowels, she finished abruptly before she could drip. Stepping back, she retied her trousers feeling much better. It had been a messy experience to learn, but such things were necessary when men were around.

Feeling ten times better, she returned to the table and took a long, deep drink. It sent her into a coughing fit as her lungs protested against the intrusion of ale, having swallowed the wrong way. The coughing fit, while mild, sent her to her knees as they gave out from absolute exhaustion. Leaning her forehead against the floor, she coughed until her lungs were appeased.

Cracking open her protesting eyes, she reached up to the table to grab a hunk of bread and a wedge of cheese and mindlessly crawled toward an abandoned cot. Pushing her body onto it, she curled around her food and fell asleep without eating them, but kept them close…just in case.

Ed woke reluctantly to the sound of thumping.

Bleary eyed, she unfurled from her ball and looked around. She almost didn't remember where she was, but the lantern was still burning which helped her to bring the room into focus. Clutched against her chest, she found the cheese and bread and immediately began shoving pieces into her mouth. She was starving again. What time was it anyway? How much time had passed?

Pushing herself into a sitting position, she swung her legs out and off of the bed as she chewed. Her eyes locked onto the table in the center of the room. Since the ale was gone, thanks to her overkill, her mouth was dry. The thumping noise came again and she glanced toward the sliding door. Someone seemed to be banging against it. Was it time to get up already? She knew that she could easily have slept longer if she hadn't been interrupted.

She finished the food and acknowledged the person knocking. "Coming." Quickly, she crossed to the chamber pot to make use of it one more time. She didn't know what the day might hold for her. She suspected meeting up with Brock and hunting down the animals that were loose would be an all-male priority; and who knew when she'd get another chance to go. Afterwards, Ed stretched her back muscles and rolled her neck.

Moving to the door, she slid it open, and jumped back when a figure fell to the floor inside the door. Squinting to make it out, she realized that it was Barlowe. "Have too much to drink or what?" Ed allowed herself a laugh, but then stopped as her new wounds compounded with old ones made the movement painful. She looked past the door and wasn't overly surprised to see that it was still dark out considering how tired she still was. She might have gotten a few hours in, but it was hard to tell. It seemed as though the rain had stopped though.

"Know where I can find Mr. Swicker?" She was walking from the room when Barlowe grabbed a hold of her boot, scratching at it like he wanted to burrow his fingers into her foot. Frowning down at him, she shook his grip off and moved away from him to get a better look.

He was groaning at her from the ground, his mouth working as if trying to talk to her and his eyes roaming her body. The sight gave her goose bumps and she walked away from him down into the stables. It hadn't occurred to her earlier, but it was odd that there were any cattle or horses in the stables, just the smell of wet hay. Had the group of men taken all the horses for the hunt? They obviously weren't back yet or they would have found her holed up in their accommodations for the night.

The stalls were all darkened since there were no lights lit in the stables. Spotting a box full of ready-to-use torches meant for the grounds, she pulled one up and crossed back into the room. Barlowe lay on the floor unmoving as she walked around him. Opening the lantern, she let the end touch the flame inside. If she was going to walk around, she'd need to be able to see. The lantern was dying anyway and she had no way of knowing where additional candles were to keep it lit.

Leaving Barlowe in his drunken stupor, she exited the stables and crossed the courtyard and began lighting the torches along some of the structures so that she could see better. The carriage was gone and the door to the manor was still open, looking dark and creepy inside. Something just didn't seem right about the place. She didn't see any lights lit through the windows there either. Wouldn't somebody have lit the lights themselves? There was no one to be seen, which struck her as just as odd as when they'd first arrived. Where was Swicker? For that matter, where was Brock?

Avoiding the front door she moved along the courtyard and walked off toward the gardens with their tall hedges, lighting torches to see along the way. She had no intentions of going into them, since they served no purpose, but a noise behind her made her turn and look back the way she'd come. Barlowe stood in the stable's doorway. Cocking an eyebrow, she was about to call out an insult in his direction about being drunk on the job when something odd shocked her.

Jaw dropping, she took a step forward and was confused with what she saw. Then, realizing he was watching her, she turned and ran into the gardens without a word. Did she just see what she thought she saw? She wanted to drop the torch, but it was the only way that she could see where she was going so she continued to run, flame sputtering as she did so.

Her mind raced as the horror of the situation fell over her. *What the bloody hell was going on around here?* She wondered. Barlowe's stomach had been torn out, and most of the left side of his face—that had been completely hidden from her before—had been missing. Thick ropy insides had been spilling from the hole in his gut and his neck was crooked as if it'd been broken. She'd seen plenty of dead bodies in her life to know that Barlowe should not be upright, let alone standing in a doorway watching her like that. There was no way. She'd seen corpses with lesser injuries who'd met their maker. Barlowe was far worse off. Her instinct had warned her when they arrived that something was wrong, but she'd forgotten it in a haze of sleep and food.

She cringed when she remembered him grabbing onto her boot earlier. Had he been trying to ask for help and she shook him off? She felt no remorse for the man since she had no real liking of him, but the idea that she hadn't even noticed his condition bothered her. She ran past the middle of the garden unable to marvel, as was intended, at the small prayer chapel that had been built there. Darting past it, she found another path leading away from the center and out into another path. Here she was, running again. After tonight, she was done with this twisted whole place. This was the last time that she would step a foot in or around Lock's Landing.

When she met a dead end of shrubs, she skidded to a halt and swore at the greenery. Who built something like this? Did rich people sit around and dream up ways to keep from getting bored? Oh, let's build a game where no one can get out. Brilliant idea. She hoped that she could meet these people to tell them what a stupid idea it was. Heart pounding in her throat, she back-tracked long enough to choose a new one and to realize that Barlowe was chasing after her. She hadn't been sure at first, but there was no mistaking it now. Ed wasn't able to tell how quickly he was able to move, but the grunting and groaning sounds that he made announced his presence within the gardens. A place he shouldn't have been able to get to with those kinds of wounds.

At least he's noisy, she consoled herself. *I can hear him coming.*

Heart racing, she reached the end of the gardens and burst out of them wondering if this whole week had been punishment for poaching bodies and selling them to a sawbones. It had been nothing but one bad moment to the next and now she was being chased by, from what she could tell, a dead man. Perfect. Really, she could now go and find a job telling fanciful tales to visitors who traveled along the sea at this rate. And people still wouldn't believe her.

Ed ran toward a large tree and braced against it trying to catch her breath, watching the garden. Would he find the way out or stay trapped in there? When a wall of shrubs began to shake like it was in a windstorm, she shook her head realizing that Barlowe was trying to walk directly through the hedge instead of following the path to reach her. The thought hadn't crossed her mind, but at the way he beat at the hedge, she wondered if it'd really been an option anyway.

Pushing past the tree, she saw that there was no way to get back to the front of the courtyard, and that the manor ran in a straight wall along the land. Her only option would be to go the way she'd come or follow the wall along the back of the manor and hope for an entrance to get inside. Running along the wall seemed to be the wisest decision currently, seeing as though she didn't want to get into a fight with a dead man.

The wall continued on and it seemed like she ran forever. Every once in a while she would almost seem to catch a glimpse of someone in a window as she passed, torch in hand. At one point, she heard the sound of breaking glass but did not stop to investigate. She didn't dare.

Sweat ran in rivulets down her back as she finally came to a corner. She quickly followed along the back side of the manor and saw a door with a wood awning over it. Ed sagged in relief and went to it, her legs feeling as though they might give out. Reaching the door, she tugged on it. It came open easily in her hand but she jumped back in shock as two bodies fell out through the door at her.

It looked as if they had reached the door on the inside, intent on making it outside, and almost made it when they had been attacked. The person doing the attacking resembled what Barlowe had looked like except she was missing an entire arm and her chest was ripped open. Bloody strips of flesh and clothing hung limply as Ed was able to see the makings of ribs.

Her feast was a tall man that looked to be in his twenties who was missing most of the right side of his face. Somehow, through the deadly onslaught, he seemed to reach out for her, begging for help. Ed stumbled backwards and almost tripped over her own feet. The smell rolling off them was clogging her nose. Sweat and blood mingled like a thick soup. That's when she noticed that two more figures were running toward her from the corner of the manor; Barlowe and another person that she didn't recognize.

Ed groaned and turned, forcing herself run away from the door and the figures striding toward her while she heard terrified yelping from somewhere behind her. She didn't dare turn around and look.

She ran straight into the manor's backyard, running along stone walkways and lush grass that she could feel under her boots. Ed had come to Lockland because she was told these were animal attacks. Swicker had told her that he didn't know what kind of attacks they were and she felt heinously mislead. His round about, almost cryptic explanation at The Slaughtered Lamb hadn't indicated that the attacks were of a human nature. Had Swicker known about this all along? If he had, had he brought her there to deliver her to the monsters that roamed the estate? Maybe he hadn't known. After all, he had supposedly gone inside the estate...

Suddenly her feet faltered and she nearly tripped face first. The carriage was gone. If Swicker hadn't known what was happening, had he taken one look inside and hopped back into the carriage and taken off? Maybe Barlowe had already been bitten and couldn't drive the carriage himself and Swicker had taken it and bolted. The bastard! Had he intentionally left her there to die or forgotten all about her?

Ed stopped to catch her breath again, glancing at the torch. The thing had saved her life. If she hadn't been able to see what had happened to Barlowe and been able to see to get away, she would have been taken down by either him or someone else. That much was obvious. Saved her life and made her a target at the same time.

Switching hands, she noticed that something caught a reflection of the torch light ahead. Having nothing to lose by checking it out, she moved forward and inspected the source. It was a symbol like one she'd seen earlier on the carriage. A Lockette family symbol. It seemed to be carved into a hill. Moving closer, she realized that no, it wasn't carved into the hill, it was a metal doorway leading into the hill. Was this a family burial plot? Ed had heard from Brock that there were some rich families that constructed large monuments to bury relatives in, but she'd never seen one before.

Ed bent to get a closer look at some foot traffic before the door, brushing her fingers over the ground. Someone had been here as recently as a few days time judging from the deep imprints that had survived the rain.

She tread carefully around the immediate perimeter, lighting her steps with the glow of the torch, looking for anything out of the place. She didn't know if burial sites were booby-trapped or not. She'd always assumed that she wouldn't be in one and had never stopped to ask Brock what to look for. Spotting something in the short grass, she stooped to retrieve it. Pursing her lips, she looked at it in the light. A ball from a pistol. Shrugging, she let the ball drop to the ground since she wouldn't need a single bullet for a pistol that she didn't possess.

Like the gardens, she hadn't planned on going inside the burial tomb with the danger surrounding her, but the sounds of moaning that was creeping closer made her rethink it. Reaching out, she pulled on the metal door and it creaked as it opened for her. Stale air gusted out from the blackness in front of her and the torch flickered in response.

Stepping forward, she felt the cold air from the crypt against her face and she held the flame before the blackness. It was bloody dark down there. Swallowing, Ed saw that the doorway led downward into a narrow set of stone steps. Nothing dangerous rushed out at her like Ed half expected, which was a good sign. Pushing the torch forward, she watched the flames as they burned away the fragile webbing that had coated parts of the entrance; either burning the crawling bugs that dwelled there or sending them fleeing from the fire.

Watching some of those fleeing black blobs in the torchlight, Ed hurried inside and closed it behind her. It was her hope that the builder of this burial site had built some kind of passage way that might lead her back to the manor. She'd been in a rich house pretending to be a maid before and had discovered a tunnel leading from the stables to the house. It'd allowed her to steal pretty well from the place and escape before she was found out.

The grounds might be overrun with things like Barlowe, but if the passage was clear underground it would be a safer way back to where she started and maybe even a hiding place until she figured how to get herself out of this mess.

Immediately, she was struck by how cold it was inside and her skin broke out in goose bumps. Moving forward, Ed held the torch and her breath as she descended the stone steps. They were narrow, thin, and steep. She silently begged herself not to fall down them. As a precaution to keep her balance, she slid a hand along the stone wall, stepping down the stairs sideways until she reached the bottom. Her boots scraped lightly against the stone as she descended. The room seemed surprisingly dry with no musty wet smells emerging from the blackness beyond the torch like she would have expected. No water must have gotten inside.

At the bottom of the steps she found a dry torch in the wall and she raised her flame to light it. It was a big space. If it weren't a touch too creepy of a thought she figured she could live in the one room alone and be relatively happy with it. Cool against the summer air, dry—no rain seepage—it seemed almost perfect.

The idea that she was actually thinking of it made her shiver. She might dig up dead people for money, but she wasn't as sure that she wanted to live with them and likely far too long dead to make a profit from it.

The room Ed was in was large, bare, and oblong, as if to prepare or view an open coffin before proceeding further inside with a darkened hallway branching out from it, opposite from where she stood.

Spotting a second torch, she crossed and lit that as well. She wasn't afraid of the dark, but it made no sense to rut around in the dark for no reason. It was difficult to tell how far the burial chamber was by looking at it. It could be merely two antechambers, but bigger families probably had decent sized areas, so it could go on quite a bit before reaching the end.

Ed stepped forward into the hallway and scanned the floor as she moved along it. No scat, no blood markings, and no dead animal bodies. It looked fairly untouched by what was going on outside. The stone hall was throwing off a chill that she could feel through her shirt as she walked quietly down it. It was getting uncomfortably cold.

She walked down the rest of the length down the hall that deposited into another room. This room held stone coffin holes in it but no coffins in them. It appeared as if the room was prepared for the more recently deceased, which likely meant that the older relatives of the family would be back through other corridors. She lit another torch holder as she passed through the room.

As she reached the end of the hallway that lead into another chamber, she pulled up short, cocking her head and listening. She could have sworn she just heard whimpering. She listened again. Wait, there it was again, quiet, almost sob-like whimpers.

As she emerged in the next large chamber she was assailed by the smell of rich copper. Blood. She held the torch high but much of the chamber was still shrouded in darkness. She noticed the coffin holes on the left side of the room were partially filled with coffins and the holes that had been filled; the coffins had all been broken open. Bones and wood were spread across the dusty floor. The damage looked old. Where was the smell of blood coming from?

Pivoting, she ignored the next chamber's entryway and crossed in the center of the room to inspect the other side, when the torches light revealed the source of the bloody odor. She froze. It took everything she had not to scream. She was not a screamer and yet...

She had seen some terrible wounds in bodies before. Men accidentally shot in the face, men caught in man-made traps, men gored and sewed up but most of them had been dead before she got there. Even Barlowe wasn't like this. Nothing came close to the live body in the state that it was now.

She stared, unable to move, the torch trembling in her hand. Her mind screamed to escape, but where to?

There was a bloody body slung over a slab where a coffin was meant to sit. It was unmistakably male, noting the heavy arms that were sprawled over the sides of the stone. Horrific long strips of skin and deep thick muscle had been noticeably torn from parts of his arms leaving a gruesome discovery for the torchlight. Thick blood from his wounds, looked black, and had run in dark rivets, pooling at the back of his head. Parts of his face had been bitten or chewed away. His lips, eyes, nose, and ears were simply gone, leaving nubs of bloody tissue behind.

His waistcoat had been shredded exposing the chilling sight of his chest. Thick curly chest hair was sticking out from where he still had patches of skin, whereas the rest was a bloody mess of exposed roped muscle and holes that leaked blood which had crusted onto his abdomen, and soaked into his trousers. His belly looked as though someone had put a fist through it and widened the hole as the large cavity wound had begun to spill out soft pink guts. Ed realized with further horror that the man's legs were missing below his knees. She moved the torch closer and saw only gristle, thick clots, and sticky wet blood on the dirty floor. Something had bitten through his leg bones and had carried them off. She shuddered, choking back burning bile in her throat, looking around for the stubs.

Movement from his thighs pulled her focus back up from his missing legs. Something was moving freely beneath the remains of his trousers. A low keening sound came from the man's throat and his jaw flapped uselessly. Hearing a high-pitched squeak, she lifted the torch and saw that rats had come from somewhere, scurrying around his head, and they were eating through his tangled frizzy hair. It left little to the imagination to what was working not so carefully beneath his trousers.

The sharp rat teeth had not broken into his brain cavity yet from what Ed could see, but they looked on the verge of it. They worked fast as she watched, as if they had no choice but to eat quick and run away. Bloody skin and hair were being chewed with gusto.

She commanded her legs to move but they didn't. She could only mutely stand and stare in complete horror, the meal of bread and cheese that she'd eaten earlier rising so threateningly in her throat. Her mind screamed at her to put the man out of his misery. There was no going back from what he was experiencing and the torment he'd endured as horrific as it was, was going to last as the rats ate his brain out of his skull. She knew what she had to do, and her hand shook as she reached for the cheese knife in her pocket. She could walk away from many things, but she could not take the suffering of this nameless man in front of her. His torment was beyond imagination.

She took a deep swallow and forced herself to step closer to the body and the strong smell of human feces caught her nose. Her belly rolled painfully and she breathed through her mouth, not blaming him for fouling himself considering the terribly slow death that he was experiencing. It'd be hard for anyone not to under the circumstances. "I'm sorry." She whispered in the general direction of where his ear would be if he still had one. She had no idea who the man was or if he'd also come in looking for a place to hide and had been attacked so horribly, but her grief for him was new to her. If the roles were reversed, she'd hope someone would do her the favor that she was bestowing on him. It was the only right thing to do.

The body froze and then bucked around as if he was finally aware someone was there. In his state, it was probably true. His head moved wildly as he realized help was in reach, but he was too far-gone to realize, there was no helping what remained of his body. How he'd survived so far was beyond her.

"I'll put an end to your pain," she promised. *This is necessary. It is an end to the agony*, she reminded herself.

She put the knife to his throat and she heard a rasp leave his throat before she cut deep, pushing the dull blade as hard as she could as she sliced. "Unnnnn."

What remained of his blood gushed out from the new open wound drenching the stone slab he lay on. The rats squeaked in his trousers as his body spasmed and jerked in death. The churning in her stomach was too much and, bracing her hands on her knees, she bent forward and threw up. Chunks of undigested bread and cheese littered the floor supported by the ale and bile that it floated in. She felt the weakness from the action tickle at the backs of her knees as they threatened to buckle, but she managed to stay on her feet. Sweat broke over her body and she wiped her mouth on the sleeve of her shirt.

Belly sensitive to already having vomited, she caught a fresh smell as the remainder of bowels that the man had released upon his death, hit her nose. Her body buckled as she dry-heaved for a moment. She urged her feet to move backwards away from the combined scents around the body. Straightening, Ed gulped, feeling the coldness of the crypt on her hot, sweaty face. She replaced the knife and tightened her grip on the torch when she caught a new odor in the air.

Now what? This place bloody sucks, why did I come down here? I should have kept running.

Turning away from the body to inspect the new source of smell, she screamed in shock and confusion when she saw what had come up behind her while she'd been tending to the helpless, tortured man. An armless rotting figure had shambled up behind her. Half of the flesh of his face was gone and she was staring into a gooey orb-less eye socket. The man's flesh had begun to bubble around his neck with gas and hang droopy from his chin. The nose had been torn away and suddenly, she was screaming into the nose hole when it leaned forward, and bit into the fleshy section of her cheek.

Shock dulled part of her senses for a moment, but then the gnashing, pulling pain of teeth digging into her cheek exploded with a white starburst in front of her eyes. She continued to scream as she brought the end of the torch up and began hammering the things back with it. She sent the flaming end along the back, setting the tattered clothing it wore on fire. As the flames quickly spread, Ed worried that the thing would stay stuck to her and catch her on fire as well.

Holding the torch over its back. She could smell a thick, fatty smell of skin starting to burn and ignored it as she grabbed for the knife again. Ed began stabbing the thing in the face, nearly lancing herself with it as she jerkily homed in on her target.

"Let go!"

Then suddenly, the thing did let go, as she pummeled its face into ruin with her swings. It dropped to the ground at her feet, on fire. She jumped away from it, blood streaming down her face. Was her cheek still there? Had it bitten or pulled a chunk away? She had no time to check.

Torch and blade in hand, she swiveled trying to make a risk assessment of the situation. Across from her, the tunnel that she hadn't explored yet, made her jump where she stood. More of the same kinds of things were watching, standing there as if curiously waiting for her next move. They were as tall as a human man, but were all rotten and putrid looking. Complete parts of their bodies were missing. Some arms were missing at the elbow or shoulder. Gore ran freely from open wounds and she could swear she saw mold growing from one of the things' eyeballs. There were some that looked almost mummified and there were half a dozen dressed fresher ones squeezed together just beyond her. On the ground, she saw some had no lower bodies and they dragged themselves with their arms. They didn't look human.

Startled, she heard rats shriek and she spun to watch in shock as one of the things had slunk up to the newly dead body and now pulled a struggling, bloody rat off and shoved it head-first into its mouth, tearing the top off. Blood and fur spurted from its lips as it chewed, moaning in its mangled throat. Two others had shambled to the same man and had begun feasting openly on his body. His belly had been completely torn open, intestines dangled, still attached to his body. Eager hands sought more of his soft warm innards as blood trickled from the open hole. Gagging, she shifted her eyes and saw the pile of rags she'd caught on fire, on the floor. The thing was still twitching, but was no longer trying to eat her. Seeing it, gave her an idea. To burn them all. She spun back at the crowd in the tunnel where some had managed to come further out of it toward her.

Shouting at them as loud as she could, the sound echoing off the walls, Ed picked out an older looking one that appeared wrapped in fragile rags and hurled the torch at it. She watched for a moment as it immediately caught on fire, which quickly spread to others next to it. The things around it moaned, trying to move away from the flames. Ones not on fire moved around the calamity while some walked right through it, catching fire in the process also.

Her face stung and she could feel the wetness of her blood glide down her face. She had to get back to the entrance. Gripping the knife in her fist, she spun and ran. A horde of the dead groaned in unison as they followed after her, dragging their rotting bodies as they gave a determined chase. The newest dead were the fastest and she heard them closer behind her, grunting and moaning, trying to get her. The smell of rot clung heavy in her nose, and her face felt ruined as the air penetrated it while she ran.

She reached the first antechamber, gasping for breath, and glanced around. She could hear the things behind her moaning collectively and knew they were not far behind her. She stared up at the door and was torn as she heard something banging on it from the other side. Barlowe?

Swallowing and blade in hand, she went for one of the torches in the room, as the moans and dragging sounds grew closer. "Bloody hell."

This is seriously going to hurt, she thought as she backed up the stairs and tried to go over how she was going to escape. Both ways were blocked. She could possibly throw the metal door open, surprising Barlowe and knocking him down as she fled. It seemed the best possible chance as she watched the dead people shamble closer.

Ed moved up another step intent on reaching the door before the things caught up to her. She hissed between clenched teeth at the jarring sensation in her cheek as she climbed the stairs. She was about half way up them, stride set in grim determination, when there was a new sound coming from deeper in the hall.

The grinding sounds of hand to hand battle. Were the dead fighting over who would reach her first? Losing momentum, she turned and watched with astonishment as the dead people that had given chase were being attacked themselves! Something white, lean, and limber leapt from the hall where they'd the group had emerged from and landed on a crawling torso crushing its skull into the stone below. Growling, the new creature lashed out with hands that had enormous claws sporting from the tips of its fingers, ripping into a walking dead man whose face was missing. A loud gaseous noise split the air as grey intestines spilled out of the opening and tumbled down the mans legs.

Unencumbered by the disembowelment, the dead man opened his mouth wide and lunged at the white creature. The creature side stepped the oncoming attack and leapt into the air, landing on the dead man. Ed watched with sickened fascination as the white creature began hacking at the dead man's neck with its sharp claws. Dead clumps of flesh flew, sticking to other dead people as it was separated.The dead man snapped his jaws and tried to move in to sink its teeth into the creatures flesh but it kept missing. The creature hacked and slashed until the dead man fell in a heap, unmoving, and decapitated onto the ground. A putrid smell floated in the air as the white creature seemed to celebrate its victory and throw itself onto a new dead victim. It took Ed a moment to realize that this was happening all around her. Claws streaked through the air and hacked while the clicking sound of dead men's teeth bounced through the room.

One track minded in their desires as they were, some of the dead people still tried to slowly reach her on the stairs. The ones at the front hadn't yet begun to understand that the group was being attacked from behind and were being set upon the new creatures.

Covering her face with the crook of her elbow to avoid the smell of rotten open wounds, Ed looked closer at the new...white, naked people?

No, they weren't people. She couldn't place them with anything other than the form of a human man, but they were badly misshapen, gaunt, strong, and seemed to mostly utilize four limbs like an animal might. What are those things?

Even as she stood and watched as mayhem took place all around her, she couldn't believe what she was seeing. Two types of creatures that she had never even heard about before today were locked in a death match in front of her. It looked like one clan fighting to exterminate another as each side fought against each other.

The white creatures were clearly waging war and appeared to be winning. Flashes of their nude bodies stood out among the drab colors of the dead people as they struggled and wrestled together. Some beat the dead peoples heads in with fists and feet, effectively caving in their skulls and spilling their brains out, while others used their considerable sharp claws aimed at the throat for decapitation. Ed noticed that with these kinds of wounds, the dead people did not get back up and the white creatures began attacking a new target in some kind of empowered frenzy. Some of the creatures gleefully chortled in their throats as if they were getting extreme satisfaction.

Ed cringed as a white creature got too close to her when it lashed out at a nearby dead person. Cheeks and chins too large for their faces, eyes sunk into their heads, teeth black, rotten, and missing, flat ear holes, and hairless. Their bodies had little fat on them and bones and muscles looked tight under the skin. Their skin tone wasn't as pure white as she'd first thought either. Many of the creatures' flesh were marred with oddly large purple and red looking sores that were being broken as they fought.

Captivated by the scene, one of the creature's large claws slashed across Ed's hand where she held the torch up to see. Yelping and cursing herself for a fool, she dropped the torch, and fell back onto the stairs. Bracing herself for a fight she knew that she couldn't win, she was shocked when the thing looked impassively at her, carefully avoided the flame, and moved onto the next dead man. Virtually ignoring her vulnerability. Ed's mind spun as she watched mutely as the dead people stumbled into the flames of the torch and were set on fire.

Ed hollered when she felt sets of hands grasp her upper arms and pull her backwards up the stairs. Kicking and flailing her arms with blood from the cut on her hand splattering the steps, she continued to fight, feeling the steps bumping against her back, creating fresh bruises.

"It's me! Young Ed, it's Mr. Swicker." He set her down and shook her forcefully with his grip and made her look into his eyes. Then Swicker's gaze flickered to the massacre happening below them and his eyes widened. "What in the bloody Hell is going on down there?"

Launching herself away from the doorway and Swicker's tight grip, Ed saw Barlowe's body unmoving in the grass. She was about to shout when she noticed that someone had separated his arms, a leg, and his head from his body. Relieved, Ed crumpled forward and braced her hands on her knees to catch her breath. She waved a hand at Swicker, explaining for him to talk first. Before she revealed what she'd seen, she wanted to know where he'd been and how he'd found her.

"When I parted company with you, I went in search of Lord and Lady Lockette. The manor was in a poor state of ruin and as I investigated, I saw many open doors with no one inside the rooms. I fear that had I walked into some of them when they'd been full, not realizing what was happening, I may have shared Mr. Barlowe's fate when he went into the kitchens." Swicker glanced at Barlowe's body. "I came upon some of these crazed people and managed to fight some of them off. I found Lady Lockette in a room on the second floor and we managed to stay safe even after some of those people chased me up the stairs. I went to the window and waited. When I saw you emerge from the stables tonight calling so much attention to yourself, I knew you were going to be in trouble. I tried to call to you, but you didn't hear me. Then I saw Mr. Barlowe follow you, which seemed impossible since he died last night."

"I slept an entire day?" Ed furrowed her brow. "Where did the carriage go?"

Swicker gestured to the people who'd been standing in the darkness not far from him, with his hands. Ed's gaze flickered to them and hoped they weren't dead people. She didn't know if she had the strength to save herself at this point. "It seems as though Lady Lockette arranged for personal transportation and sent some correspondence for grounds assistance as soon her husband grew ill from an attack he'd had, which is how I became involved. She called for men to arrive for a hunt. When the men I sent ahead of me arrived, they walked into a slaughter. We didn't see these crazed people when we first arrived because they were busy chasing those poor fellows through the manor.

"Lady Lockette's cousin, Mr. Irwin Fairchild, came to the estate to take her away to her family's home based on the information he'd received in the letter about the animal attacks. Using the window, he met with us where we were barricaded in. After we came up with a plan, with great peril to himself, he left and hid the carriage further down the way so that we'd have a safe method of escape. His own horse was attacked when he first arrived.

"When I saw you I knew it was time to make our move. I brought you here, lad, and I'm responsible for putting you in harms way. Some could live with just walking away, but not I. When we reached the courtyard, we followed the path you'd taken. Then when we were close enough, we heard Mr. Barlowe striking the door to the crypt, we knew you would be in here."

Ed felt sweat dot her forehead as her legs gave out and she finally fell heavily onto the ground. She didn't like being beholden to any man, but if her strength had allowed it she might have just kissed his boots. She was a lowly street boy for all that he knew but he'd taken the risk to rescue her anyway with these dead people running around. A selfless gesture of which she'd never had before. Brock may have saved her hide before, but always to the tune of being partners who made money together. Never just because her life had been in danger. Brock had a stake whether she lived or died. Swicker had not, and yet he'd come for her.

She thought that he'd taken an opportunity and had left her on her own. She was used to the familiar sting of abandonment. It'd made for a hard life, but one that had gotten her this far.

The idea that she hadn't been betrayed and left behind after all made her feel uncomfortable in her chest so she coughed and spoke. "With Mr. Barlowe following me, I just ran. I knew something wasn't right about him, being messed up like he was." Ed sucked on her teeth and made a smacking noise with her lips. As she spoke, she pressed her eyes closed and fought the desire to probe the wound on her cheek. She explained what had lead her to the crypt and then to the man she'd found in the burial chamber.

"That can't be."

Ed looked up at the voice. A woman, presumably Lady Lockette, stood in a man's overcoat that covered a blood splashed corset, and a Lady's fine underwear. Her perfect doll face showed in the torchlight as she stepped forward. She scowled down at Ed as if she was something scraped off the bottom of her shoe. Next to her the tall, thin, hawk-nosed young man with curly hair, presumably Mr. Irwin Fairchild, leaned forward and nodded his agreement and placed his hand on her elbow.

"My husband's family has lived here all their lives and none of these creatures have been around until quite recently. I don't know where these things come from but things living inside the crypt? Underground? It's preposterous. I've never heard such a wild tale in all my life."

Ed grunted, hanging her head as her face stung with embarrassment and pointed toward the door. She was used to it from people like Lady Lockette, but didn't like being called a liar. "Well, where ever they came from, they're in there. Feel free to take a walk inside. I'll wait here."

Swicker made a soothing sound intent on disarming a verbal fight before one erupted. "We needn't quarrel about the particulars. It's possible these things started this whole ordeal if they were the ones that attacked Lord Lockette to begin with. Who knows how they got in there. Maybe they dug a way inside. Either way, it's a dangerous location."

Swicker kneeled, tipping Ed's face up into the light of the torch. The woman squealed and was pointing at Ed's face. Ed was about to counter with a rude comment about the Lady's choice in attire, when suddenly she wasn't standing there anymore. A long white and purple mottled arm had snaked out of the crypt door and jerked the pretty Lady Lockette inside.

Lady Lockette's screams echoed loudly down the stone stairs. Stunned and horrified at what had just happened, Ed watched Mr. Fairchild vault forward and disappear inside, his footsteps pounding hard on the stairs as he called his cousin's name, adding to the Lady's screams.

"Stay right here." Before Ed could utter a word, Swicker jumped to his feet and also flew down the stairs after them. Ed hadn't really cared that the idiot cousin had rushed down the steps after her, but her stomach knotted and turned over when Swicker disappeared down them.

Crawling on her hands and knees, Ed moved to the open doorway and stared up over the lip of the crypt. She saw the carnage in the lighting below. The dead people that had come for her were all down, laying in broken goopey grey piles on the floor. The newest casualty, Lady Lockette, lay in a bloody mess on the floor where one of the white creatures had chewed her neck clear through to the bone and was carelessly shredding through her underwear to get at her stomach contents. When the thing shifted in the light to slurp at the blood pumping from the wounds, Ed saw that the creature was pregnant.

Shuddering, her gaze sought out Swicker. He fought with a sword, winning against the one he was up against. Ed could see that he was quite good as he slashed and jabbed, and the creature howled as Swicker continued his assault. Two other creatures were taking down the cousin in a grotesque spray of blood and screams as the large claws ripped him into thick sections.

Ed touched the deep scratches on her hand remembering how sharp those things had been. The cuts stung as if she'd been slashed with knives. She didn't particularly like the hawk-nosed man's status, but she felt sorry for him as he died violently. Her gaze went back to Swicker. A valiant man who had wanted to help an orphan 'boy' from the streets, who had rushed into a dangerous dark house to check on his Lord and Lady, and a man who had rushed headlong into danger without knowing fully what he faced, to do the same a second time.

He managed to kill the one he was fighting and seriously wound another, but did not fare well against two more. His death was not kind either and Ed sat in remorse and shock as she watched when claws ripped off his face and sliced through his chest. Quietly, not wanting to see anymore, Ed dropped out of the way, reached up, and closed the door to the crypt. Numb, she leaned against it for a moment staring up at the sky as the sun was beginning to rise.

The wound in her cheek throbbed in time to the claw marks on her hand and she wondered what she would do now. Wearily pushing to her feet, she started walking aimlessly away from Lockette's land. In the distance she could hear shouting, but she didn't turn around.

She needed to get far away from the pit-stain of Lock's Landing and move on. Later, after she curled up under a pricker bush intent on sleeping, her mind would stop reeling with the events of the night and she would wonder, *what the hell happened to Brock?*

EPILOGUE

Doctor Michael Carver sat at the open window of his office as he stared blankly at the sun coming up over the trees. He'd traveled all night to get home to Lock's Landing and the trip was taking its toll on him. His eyes stung with the urgency to sleep and he was beginning to give in.

Young Reiley Todde had briefed him a few hours ago on his visitors while he'd been away. Watching the peach colors grace the sky, he rubbed his worn face. He'd rather hoped the boy, Ed, would be waiting for him.

Stretching his cramped legs first, Michael rose from the footstool and indeed decided to call it a night. Pickings for fresh bodies had been rather slow. Only two fresher ones through the entire night since he'd come in. Usually it was double or triple that amount. Not many people probably knew that he was back in town yet.

Sighing, he straightened his jacket and took a last look around. Then, loosening the fabric around his middle, he leaned forward, and pushed the shutters closed. Climbing the noisy stairs to his room above his medical practice, he undressed, and lay in bed staring at the ceiling.

He was in the business of bodies so it shouldn't shock him when one came in that he recognized. Rolling over, he fluffed his pillow and breathed in deep. It rankled him that he'd had to give coin to the Baker boys. But the criminals knew, when you brought in a body, Doctor Michael Carver would pay for it.

Michael didn't know how it happened, but he could tell by the treatment of the body that Thaddeus Brock had not died easily after being mugged, beaten, skull crushed in, stripped to his underwear, and dragged in by his feet by that band of wretched street kids. He started to wonder if he should make a rule about the bodies being *buried* first. Otherwise, he envisioned those boys bringing far more bodies in his direction after a fresh murdering spree. He needed the bodies for multiple medical practices but he didn't want to give anyone the excuse to knock off a few people in exchange for the coins. He wasn't *that* kind of man. He had standards, yes, but he wasn't a murderer.

He wondered if Ed knew. Sighing, he turned on the bed and his restless gaze caught the open letter on the bedside table next to his pocket watch. He'd been summoned to Lockland Estate because Lord Lockette had taken ill. There was no further information provided to help him determine what kind of illness that it might be. *Your presence is urgently requested.*

Michael was the closest doctor in the area. It meant that he was called upon for all manner of medical related issues. He supposed he'd get a wagon together, pack a big medical bag full of varying supplies, and make his way to the estate in the afternoon. Maybe he'd take Reiley with him. The kid could make a good apprentice if he wanted honest work.

Michael closed his eyes and let sleep take him. When he tumbled into his dreams, he dreamed of the dead.

AFTERWARD: AUTHOR'S NOTE:

Imagine a time with no cell phones or land lines. Education wasn't widespread so being able to read and write wasn't as common as it was today. Letters could take weeks or months to arrive anyway. What if someone important to you just vanished leaving no clues behind while you were left with a thin trail of information trying to find them?

Cryptic came about when I sat and wondered how hard it would have been in that kind of environment, especially carrying a secret like Ed has. I wondered what could happen if mysterious attacks weren't just a bunch of bandits in the night robbing people, but a monstrous threat above and below in a time where people could completely fall off the radar without a widespread alert system. What could happen when shoddy communication could lead to inaccurate information, whether by intent or by accident?

This is a peek behind the curtains, a snap shot in the day of the life of a few unlucky individuals. I hope that you enjoyed the tale. Thank you for reading it and if you're wondering what's going to happen to Ed now…you never know, you might see her again some day. -DAC

DEAD- the 12 book series

The unthinkable has happened.
The dead are walking!
Humanity's fragile thread may
be reaching its bitter end.
Individuals and groups struggle
to survive…some at any cost.
Will there be anybody left?
Or, is this just…
The Ugly Beginning?

The Dead Walk:

Samuel Todd is a regular guy:
...Failed husband...
...Loving father...
...Dutiful worker...
...Aspiring rock star.
He had no idea if anyone
would care, or take the time,
to read his daily blog entries
about his late night observa-
tions. But what started as an
open monologue of his day-to-
day life became a running
journal of the first-hand ac-
count detailing the rising of
the dead and the downfall and
degradation of mankind...

Catch all 3 books in the Zomblog Trilogy

Bennie L. Newsome

You can run, but you can't hide from...

the
BoogeyMann

**THIS IS
THE END**

ERIC POLLARINE

IN THE ARMS
OF NIGHTMARES

ROBERT DEAN

GRUESOMELY
Grimm
ZOMBIE
Tales
volume one
For the not so young

Wilhelm & Jakob Grimm
and JW Brown

DAKOTA
BY TODD BROWN

FERVOR

CHANTAL BOUDREAU

MAGIC
UNIVERSITY

CHANTAL BOUDREAU

Stories Around the Campfire
With Uncle Eric

By
Eric Pollarine

Anthologies from MDP

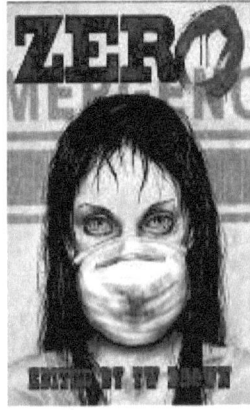

LOOK CLOSELY
THESE ARE DRAWINGS, NOT PICTURES

MAY DECEMBER
Publications

**The growing voice in horror
and speculative fiction.**

Find us at www.maydecemberpublications.com
Or
Email us at contact@maydecemberpublications.com

DA Chaney is the author of her first short stories in *First Time Dead 2* and *Hell Hath No Fury*. She is also a horror movie reviewer for *Altered Realities Radio* and for *The G.A.S.P Factor* online. When she isn't writing or planning her next story, she is reading or checking out movies in Western Massachusetts. You can get in touch with her on her Facebook Page: DA Chaney or on Twitter as: DA_Chaney.

www.ingramcontent.com/pod-product-compliance
Lightning Source LLC
Chambersburg PA
CBHW030612130626
46552CB00002B/525